I0629786

A Dangerous Liaison

Descent Into Chaos

by

Leslie LeBlanc

POD Publishing

Author: Leslie LeBlanc

NB, Canada

Cover Art by - <u>selfpubbookcovers.com/woofie_2015</u>

Chapter One

Cassidy

Her heels echoed off the laminate floor as she searched for room 306. If security hadn't miss-spelled her name on the appointment sheet, tardiness wouldn't have been an issue. It seemed an eternity before Sergeant Major Mercer answered their call and gave the OK for her to proceed.

Cassidy Macayla didn't understand the summon. Employed by a small-scale security company she worked concerts, office buildings. Nothing worthy of attention from the US army. She never realized her boss was friends with the Sergeant Major, but when asked for a suitable candidate for the job, Jim chose her.

A sigh of relief escaped upon finding the room and she startled when coming face-to-chest with a burly statue of a man.

"I was about to go find you." The man's thick, baritone voice was calming. Short salt-and-pepper hair adorned his head and a hint of age lines softened the hard edge of his face. If she were to guess his age, likely forty-five, not over fifty. A smile swept across his face. Hazel eyes sparkled with intelligence.

"No need."

Traitorous honey-blond strands escaped her loose bun. Tucking them behind an ear she coughed nervously and straightened. He stepped aside, took his seat, adjusting his uniform as she sat across his polished wooden desk.

"I apologize, Sir, err, Sergeant."

"Right. Let's get to it. Do you know why you're here?"

"No Sir. Sorry. I fail to see any qualifications I possess that would be of military interest."

He reached into a desk drawer, pulled out a file, and read from it.

"Training in Adult/Child/Infant CPR, AED Certification and First Aid at a professional level. Level 3 handgun training. Mixed martial arts training... Just to name a few." Mercer let out an impressed whistle. "Quite a list of attributes for someone working out of such a small outfit."

She squared her shoulders. Was that information really so important?

"Can't be too prepared. Should at least be ready to render aid to any injured. That, and I try to make myself indispensable." She kept her tone serious.

He gave a slight nod.

"I see. He wasn't joking about your professionalism."

She crossed her legs, folding her hands over a knee, waiting for him to get to the point. The army wanting anything from her was enough to set her anxiety into overdrive, but she forced an air of calm. She was a nobody. Always had been, always would be.

"I assume he was also serious about your ability to uphold absolute confidentiality."

She raised an eyebrow. Oh, she could keep a secret, several she'd take to the grave.

"I'm certain there's someone more suitable among your ranks."

He gently tossed the folder on the desk before him.

"Actually, we need someone with no affiliation with us or any governing agencies. One of our men got injured while on a mission and needs assistance through his recovery."

Cassidy frowned.

"This sounds more appropriate for a licensed care assistant."

"Not quite. Due to the incident and nature of his mission, and possible problems that may arise from it, all your skills may be necessary."

She tensed. This sounded dangerous. *Way* above her pay rate.

"If I'm to risk life and limb, shouldn't I know more?" He appeared to deliberate before answering.

"He was returning from an intelligence mission when attacked. We're not sure the details yet but suspect a double-cross. The explosion that ensued left him injured and with amnesia. He's lucky to be alive. Until we catch whoever is responsible, and he regains his memory, we need him under watch, kept safe. Because we don't know who's responsible, we need someone under the radar. That's you."

She squirmed.

"I see... What if I refuse?"

The notion clearly displeased him.

"We'll compensate you handsomely for your trouble."

Trouble? Talk about an understatement. She didn't like the risks associated with this job, but with her mother in a coma and nobody else willing to help, saying 'no' wasn't really affordable. She sighed.

His unmistakable confidence of her acceptance unnerved her. Did he find out her mother was having medical issues? Impossible. She didn't tell Jim about her mother, only family and two best friends. Perhaps he was a gambler of sorts.

"To sum it up you're hiring me as a sitter, care assistant, and bodyguard?" The very idea of anyone in the military needing a bodyguard had her resisting the urge to laugh hysterically.

His lips pressed into a thin line.

"This is top secret. The return of his memory is of vital importance. He's been receiving medical treatment for his wounds but isn't fully recovered, and his amnesia is still an issue. His seizures need monitored as well. You must keep in direct contact with me."

He handed her a folded slip of paper from the breast pocket of his uniform.

"This is my number. I expect daily updates."

She accepted the number. Her stomach tightened picturing her mother lying immobile, hooked up to a cluster of machines. Given her circumstances she had little choice. What's the worst that could happen?

"Fine, assuming you're serious about the compensation."

He gave a firm nod.

"Better than what Jim's paying you, by far."

This had disaster written all over it.

"So, when do I meet this person?"

"Now."

He pushed a button on the phone on his desk and a female voice responded.

"Yes, Sir?"

"Please send Special Agent Averey to my office."

"Yes, Sir."

Heavy footsteps approached, a slight limp audible. Mercer ushered him in.

"Thank you for coming."

"No problem, Sir."

That voice, so familiar. The world stood still. When she turned, it amazed her that her jaw hadn't literally hit the floor. She forced a composed facade but her insides were chaotic. She smoothed out her navy blue, knee-length skirt as she stood.

Even after about fifteen years she couldn't forget him. He'd haunted her dreams for years, even after his joining the forces, which only served to drive a wedge between them. Despite their friendship she'd wanted him, craved him like a cat does Whiskas. Unfortunately, she'd been so far below his radar she may as well have been invisible.

Unsurprising, really. She'd always been a plain Jane, overlooked most of her life by the opposite sex. And sure, he may not be as debonair as Justin Timberlake, he still had his own unique charm, enough to capture her attention. But in a lineup of girls, she'd be the one at the end, separated from second-last by every planet between Mercury and Pluto.

His crisp, ocean-blue eyes, framed now by a few smile-lines, were as captivating as she remembered. Able to incinerate with just a look. He'd bulked up since she last saw him, yet he still maintained the mystery and commanding presence that remained part of his allure. The uniform only enhanced it.

He'd lost the hair for a military style shave, giving him a more devastating edge. He leaned on the cane for support. The evidence of injuries didn't diminish his sex appeal. Lanky or buff, he was something to behold. *Crap!* Mercer began the introduction.

"Cassidy Macayla, Special Agent Chase Averey."

He offered that unforgettable smile that made the butterflies in her stomach do the rumba. Extending her hand, she showed no indication she remembered him. She was hopeless. She couldn't be sure he remembered her, but looking foolish didn't fit into her agenda.

"Pleased to meet you, Agent Averey."

He may have been sizing her up, but his piercing gaze left a burning trail in its wake. He took her hand, shaking firmly, a glint in his eyes.

"The pleasure's mine, Mrs. Macayla."

"It's Miss." *Double crap!* Last thing she needed was him thinking her the same loser as in school, assuming he remembered. It didn't seem so. This whole 'does he or doesn't he' thing made her head ache.

"Sorry, *Miss* Macayla."

The way he emphasized her name in that deep, rich voice strummed through her insides and felt as intimate as any physical touch, far deeper than she remembered. He crooked a corner of his mouth in a cocky grin as if he knew what he was doing. She was almost certain that long lineup of women existed just outside the door. She fought the urge to swallow. This hormonal garbage was for teenagers, but when Chase looked at her, she swore the temperature rose ten degrees.

"So how far back do you remember?" She refused to give any hint of the control he exuded over her rebellious body, not that he'd care. His face took on an expression as serious as her tone, but the look in his eyes hinted at mischief.

"I don't remember any of the mission, and possibly a few months before it."

She crossed her arms. A part of her insides screamed 'I told you so!'. She feared bad things would happen to him. Something she didn't think herself able to handle. It may have been years, but she still remembered parts of that conversation.

Though she tried for calm when speaking her feelings, inside she freaked. She tried to be supportive, but it was hard. Her initial thoughts were of him missing limbs or being carted off in a bag.

He warned her they'd see and hear less of each other. While she'd fought valiantly for reason, it felt like a part of her had died. She never understood being with someone in that profession. It would be so hard to deal with and probably kill her.

"I see..."

Cassidy turned to Mercer.

"So how does this work? I follow him around until something happens? Do I prepare meals, clean, change dressings...?"

Chase winced. The pained expression lasted a split-second, but she noticed. It clawed at her. She also remembered he wasn't one to betray his emotions. If he were going through the worst problems imaginable, you'd never tell by looking at him, unless he allowed you. He'd always been a pro at that. Her expression softened. She always held a soft spot for him, the fool that she was.

"I have no idea how bad your injuries are and I need to understand what I'm doing. I'm out of my element, sorry. Don't worry, I'll do what needs done."

Mercer piped in.

"You'll stay with him and possibly help with housework. Whatever Agent Averey needs. A domestic picture helps. Until we figure out who the traitor is, Averey remains a possible target. Someone has everything to gain by keeping him forgetful and silent, or taking him out of the equation all together. We believe his home to be safe, for now."

Paint a domestic picture? Was she supposed to pretend to be his girlfriend? Oh, this was getting ridiculous.

"I see, I get to add escort and housekeeper to the list." She was ready to turn tail and run, but something in Chase's eyes held her in place. What was it about him that had her wanting to say 'yes' to almost everything? *Sucker...*

"I wouldn't say that, but the illusion of a relationship helps. Remember Cassidy, top secret. Nothing can allude to what's happening. You need to be as unassuming as possible and from the look of things, a care assistant will be less believable."

Just great... What did he mean by that? What things?

"I get it, acting, not escorting."

Problem was her reactions wouldn't be an act. This would be hard. The rational side of her screamed to stop being an idiot for letting her hormones get the better of her, but her insides protested at the unfairness of being stuck in this predicament.

"Do you have any more questions?" Mercer asked.

"Not at the moment."

Truth was, Chase's proximity clouded her head. She kept her eyes on Mercer.

"When do I start?"

It was Chase who answered.

"Right now."

Cassidy swallowed hard. With his voice, those scorching eyes and that wicked smile, he could have asked her to follow him through hell and back and she would. Hadn't she agreed to it before knowing it was for him? She'd almost bet women jumped at his every command, just at the snap of those long fingers of his. She was in way over her head.

"Anything else?"

The Sergeant Major smiled.

"No, we're done here. If anything comes up, I have your number."

Was there anything about her of which he wasn't aware? She turned her attention to Chase.

"Alright, lead the way."

Chapter Two

Chase

Chase couldn't believe his eyes. Cassidy, all grown up, toned up, and filled out in ways every man dreamed. Those emerald-green eyes never lost their sparkle, and the natural pout of her lips left him wanting a taste. A part of him wanted to rip that elastic free of those tempting blond strands.

The blazer of her matching ensemble seemed designed to draw attention to her ample chest. Her lack of ring caught his eye. Not that it mattered. Undoubtedly, someone, somewhere was going to freak after finding out her new assignment.

He remembered her alright. A sweet girl, kind, caring. When bullied in school she'd been very protective of him. A good friend.

Also thoughtful, generous. When the gang were out for an evening of fun, it was usually on her. Fiercely independent and secretive, he often wondered what she hid. It disappointed him when they lost touch. For whatever reason, he couldn't seem to see her as anything more than a just a good friend.

"Am I following or are you even allowed to drive?"

Her voice revealed nothing of whether she remembered him. He was aware that if she didn't want you knowing something, you didn't, much like himself.

He needed to sit soon. His leg burned like fire, felt as though it might explode, as did his ribs. Between the pain medication and the leg injury, driving was out of the question.

"You'll have to drive. I'll give directions."

She nodded.

"Sounds good."

She led him to her silver Lumina and waited patiently. Many people became impatient having to wait. If she was, it didn't show. She opened the passenger door, and he needed to bend awkwardly to sit. The door didn't close until he had the cane tucked between his legs. A second later she sat behind the wheel. Demi Lovato blared from the radio once the vehicle started, screaming something about a heart attack. Cassidy lowered the volume slightly.

"Anywhere you want to stop first? Hungry? Thirsty?"

Another dose of pain medication was due, and he didn't want to risk taking it on an empty stomach.

"I could eat a burger."

Tension wafted from her, recognizable any time they were alone. She erected that wall he recognized far too well. Did she always behave this way around people, or just him?

"OK. BK sound good?"

He smiled. She gave one in return. Warm, sweet, bright.

"Sure, sounds good."

Due to May's unseasonable warmth, Cassidy rolled down her window. Not a cloud in the sky, and only the gentlest breeze swept past her. With mercy she went through the drive-thru rather than make him walk inside. He'd have done it, but dreaded every step. She asked what he wanted to eat. True to memory, she insisted on paying. They pulled into a spot at a secluded part of the lot.

"If you don't mind my asking, how did you become an agent?" She swallowed a bite of burger, patiently awaiting his reply.

He didn't mind, but wouldn't give many details, especially not the worst. There was much travel, plenty of sit and wait, many interesting things and people, but when the action hit, it was intense, brutal, chaotic. Killing someone didn't just roll off your back. All the psychological recovery practices in the world didn't erase the impact, only made it tolerable... Barely.

There's much mental training, not only physical. At the basic level you have to train the mind for survival, strive for acute focus despite the chaos, be the calm amid the storm, and never forget, it's kill or be killed. That's before touching on his position as an agent.

"I worked hard, trained, and got promoted. What do you do?"

Mercer had been sketchy on the details. She didn't prompt for further explanation. He didn't know why he found that so surprising. Probably because so many people did.

"I do small fry things, concerts, business and office buildings. This is new to me."

Why would the Sergeant Major hire a woman from such a small outfit?

"Why you?"

She swallowed.

"Apparently it's preferable if you can throw a punch and fire a gun."

Something told him she was downplaying. Another skill that hadn't changed. The last bit rattled in his head.

"You carry a firearm?"

She nodded. He scanned her but didn't see where it might be hiding. She raised a brow when she caught him looking.

"It's in the glove compartment."

For all she knew he was checking her out. OK, so he did that too, but she sensed his

question. Scary. It was tempting to pick a number between one and ten.

"Did you want to have a look? I'll let you, but don't touch."

Her eyes sparkled, her lips only hinting a twitch. Was that a double entendre, or his mind playing tricks on him? She sighed, reached over, and opened the small door. An intoxicating floral scent wafted from her hair. He resisted the urge to lean forward, sure his ribs would explode if he did. Inside a velvet black cloth rested a Desert Eagle. He ran a finger across the sleek barrel. Even though she'd told him not to touch, she watched in silence. He figured she'd probably let him get away with anything.

He'd never pegged her as someone who'd throw a punch, let alone shoot someone. She withheld so many secrets it felt like she was throwing him a bone. What compelled her to take up arms?

"You got a magnum? From where?"

She finished her burger and picked up a fry.

"Ordered it from Israel."

She probably could have gotten one at any of the gun shops there in Portland. Perhaps she wanted to support their economy or some such thing. He replaced the cloth and shut the compartment door before starting on his burger, which he devoured.

He grabbed a Naproxin from the bottle in his pocket and swallowed it with a gulp of Root Beer.

"I suppose I'm in good hands. Do you carry anything else?"

She hesitated before inching up her skirt mid-thigh and pulling a switchblade from a garter. There was no stopping the heat coursing through his veins. She held it out to him. The metal retained its warmth from extended contact with her skin. Part of him wished to discover how warm she was inside. He bit his lower lip, grateful to be sitting.

"I have more, but I'll have to show you later, assuming you're still interested in seeing my arsenal."

His imagination ran away with that, parts of his anatomy followed. He forced himself to focus a moment on the intricate design etched in the handle before returning it. He rubbed his hand over the dark-blonde peach-fuzz on his head as he watched her fix her skirt. To give a cavity search was tempting.

"No, that's OK. I'm just surprised they'd send someone so small."

Her eyes shot daggers. She stood about six inches short of his five-eleven, and didn't seem like a fighter, but rather a dainty healer.

"He said he needed someone unassuming. Apparently, I fit the bill."

Holding back a chuckle was impossible. His sides ached.

"I'd say."

Her face became stoic.

"Is there anywhere else you'd like to go?"

He remembered the empty fridge calling his name. Grocery shopping had been a nightmare. Perhaps having her would be useful, he wouldn't have to bother his brother for help. He hated asking, about as much as he hated the idea of someone coming to finish him off. His independence meant everything. To rely on others for the most basic things was hard to bear, but those eyes told him he shouldn't be afraid to ask for anything.

"I do need groceries."

She reached behind the car seat and pulled out her purse. Before he knew it she offered a small notepad and pen.

"Write what you need. I'll run in and get it for you."

His jaw tensed. Last thing he needed was her treating him like an invalid. He pushed them away.

"I can do it!"

She blinked and gulped. He never meant to snap, but the stress lately had become overwhelming. Cassidy lowered her head to hide her face, but he still noticed her bottom lip tremble.

"You're right, I'm sorry. I just... The pain... Do you want me to go in with you?"

There was the sweet girl he remembered, who offered to fight his battles with him, protected him from a sucker punch by the bullies on the bus. A fact he only discovered later on.

The same girl who told him with concern that while she supported his decision to join the army, she feared for his safety. There was no hiding the sound of defeat in her voice when they spoke that night. He could have sworn it broke her heart.

Did her lip tremble that same way? *Oh Cassidy...*

He exhaled, unable to deny the thrill of knowing she remembered, or understand why it shook him to the core.

"Cassidy, it seems your professional detachment never left the office."

She gasped and her head shot up to face him. He cupped her face, running a thumb across a delicate ivory cheek. For a split-second her eyes sparkled like polished gems, only to fall into shadow. She tensed and the walls came up again. She turned, started the car.

"I'm not sure what you mean."

He retracted his hand, dejected. He shouldn't be so emotional about this, her. What was wrong with him?

"How long are we going to play this game? You remember, why pretend otherwise?"

Her forearms rested against the steering wheel, a distant expression on her face.

"I had no idea if you remembered or not. If you didn't... I... I don't know. You said nothing, and I didn't want to impose."

She swallowed.

"How'd you know I remembered?"

Their eyes met. He could keep secrets too. He smiled like the cat that ate the canary. With a shake of her head, she started for the exit.

"I'm sorry, I meant no insult by it."

His heart ached at the sadness in her voice. He ran a thumb along the delicate line of her neck for comfort, or so he told himself. She shivered and shrugged away.

"Don't touch my neck, please."

What did that mean? Was he allowed to touch other places? An enjoyable idea. He couldn't help but ask.

"Why not?"

She squirmed, eyes never straying from the road. For a moment he didn't think she'd answer. She coughed.

"Crossed wires."

His back shot straight, so fast it aggravated his ribs and searing pain shot through his chest. He'd forgotten that. When she used to tease him with some silly neck pinch thing. It was dumb, immature, and he was sure she'd known the fact, but the way her soft skin pressed the chords of his neck sent a jolt through his spine, straight to his manhood.

She was naïve then, couldn't possibly understand the effect of her touch. 'Crossed wires' was the first thing that came to mind when she inquired about his reaction. A deep-rooted need to preserve her innocence overwhelmed him. He didn't care so much when it came to other girls. Why her?

Chapter Three

Cassidy

Crossed wires. That's the only thing which came to mind. Something Chase once told her. She assumed it to be one of those phantom pain things, like if you scratch an itch on your leg only to feel a pinch on your arm or something. A part of her hoped it resulted in a different effect on him, such as the one on her just now, but that was wishful thinking. Wishes didn't come true for Cassidy.

She fought the lingering heat that simmered between her thighs and refused to spare him a glance. She gnawed at her lower lip fiercely. Pain is the cleanser, right? One might ask why still want something you can't have. The best her brain came up with was that the heart wants what it wants. Her heart needed a gag. Reason should rule, but try as she might, her body remained a traitor.

"What grocery store do you usually go to?" She asked when finally able to find her voice again.

"Trader's on Marginal."

She nodded. Cassidy had never been there, remaining faithful to her favorite, the Market on Somerset. They arrived about fifteen minutes later.

Cassidy opened the passenger side door and extended her hand but he waved it away. Understandable if he valued independence as much as she, but that didn't lessen the sting. She wanted to help.

After locking up the car, she caught up to him. The firm look of his butt beneath his camouflage pants was unmistakable. She shook her head. Window shopping mattered little to her but in that instant her self-control slipped. *Cassidy, focus!* She rubbed an arm nervously, studying him.

Whatever he took seemed to help lessen his pain, but he still leaned on that cane pretty hard. If it were possible to make his misery go away, she would, but she was no genie.

The store bustled as Moon and Back by Savage Garden blared over the speakers. Discomfort grew because it used to remind her of Chase. She fought to tune it out and spied a shady group of teens eyeing the beef jerky. She clutched her black purse tighter to her side.

People stared, especially women. A group of young ladies passed by, dressed in skinny jeans and shirts that barely covered their stomachs. Their eyes devoured him as one would a steak dinner after not eating in days.

She understood. It was clear to anyone with a working pair of eyes that Chase lacked nothing in the aesthetics department, and women loved a man in uniform. It was just as obvious she didn't hold a candle to these women. One of them twinkled her fingers at him and it took everything not to roll her eyes. *Hopeless, Cassidy, just hopeless.*

"Hi." A young brunette called in to him in a sultry voice. Her friends giggled.

He offered a flirtatious smile and nod, then continued on his way. No way could he ever be unaware of the way women looked at him. He had a type alright, and it wasn't her.

Even when it came to women, he always seemed in control. She didn't know what it was about a man in control of his faculties. There was something irresistible about that. Well, almost.

He grabbed a cart and tossed his cane in before pushing. She figured leaning on it would let him take more of the weight off his leg and a small measure of relief swept through her. They slowly proceeded through the aisles.

"Just tell me what you need and I'll grab it."

He nodded in agreement. By the time they reached the checkout counter, the cart overflowed with food. Something told her he'd been too proud to ask for help. Despite his good points, he'd always been a stubborn man, at least from as far back as she remembered, and sometimes prone to reckless and impulsive decisions.

Never would she forget when he used to run out in the middle of the road and walk the yellow line. She'd yell at him, "Get off the road before you get run over! You're going to get yourself killed!" In which he'd respond "I won't get hit, I'm right in the middle!" Meanwhile, passing motorists honked madly. He certainly pushed her buttons. Those times, she wanted to slap him.

Halfway to the car her phone rang. She rummaged through her purse until she found it. A quick glance at the caller ID and she frowned. Damn it, Steve! Why didn't he get the hint? They were over, had been for months, and this crazy stalker thing didn't make her want him more. She gulped against the lump in her throat but the thing wouldn't budge. She shut the ringer off and dropped the cell back in her purse.

"Something wrong?"

Cassidy straightened. She didn't need to discuss her problems with him. She'd always been able to handle herself.

"Nothing to worry about."

His lips pursed slightly. She offered him her brightest smile. As a child her mother told her she'd smile through the worst things imaginable. That was no lie. She smiled no matter how much pain she endured. Her whole world might be falling apart, everyone she loved gone forever, she herself could be on her deathbed, all at once, and she'd still manage to smile.

Thoughts of her mother crept in, and she fought the despair that followed. Nearly six months went by and nobody knew when, or if, she'd wake. The cost of care was astronomical and only climbing higher. How long would this continue? She'd made sacrifices galore, but it was never enough. The stress weighed heavy and since her junky brother didn't want to help, she bore the burden alone. Ever since he learned about their mother's accident, he'd made himself harder to find than Carmen Sandiego.

She found drunk driving abhorrent. It saddened her the jackass died before she killed him herself. OK, maybe not, but she had every right to be angry and upset. At least he couldn't do it again.

"I need to pick up a few things at my place."

She hoped he didn't want to follow. She lived in a small room in a three bedroom house shared with two roommates. Him seeing her shortcomings was less than desirable.

"Alright."

After she unlocked the doors and trunk, they started tossing bags in but stopped when a hiss escaped Chase's lips. His pained expression gripped her heart and squeezed, like a boa tightening around its prey. He clutched at his side while leaning on the cane so hard, it trembled beneath his weight. She gently pried the bag from his hand.

"Have a seat in the car, I'll take care of the rest."

The warring in his head was obvious as he hesitated. Never before had she seen him so vulnerable. It crushed her.

"Please." She sighed, hating to beg, but unable to bear the sight of his misery.

After another moment of hesitation he did. How would she be able to handle this? Seeing him in this condition broke her heart. Their reunion should have been a happy one, with a number exchange and invitations for pool and RockBand. Anything but this! Well, almost. Another sigh and she let the trunk lid fall shut.

The drive was short, quiet. She glanced over a couple of times but his expression warned her not to speak. Perhaps it dawned on him this was the first of many times she'd witness something he didn't want her to.

Cassidy rushed in and out in about five minutes. She didn't have much and what she did wouldn't fill half a storage locker. With the baggage in the backseat she climbed behind the wheel and turned to Chase who still looked unapproachable. She deliberated whether or not to ask. He needed to go home, eventually. She opted to wait.

Minutes ticked by and that faraway stare started to scare her. Could he be having a flashback? Was his medication making him drowsy? She needed to do something.

"Chase?"

Hesitantly, she placed a hand on his. It was warm, a bit clammy. His jolt startled her. Sharp eyes bore into her. She wanted to wrap her arms around him, comfort him until his problems went away, instead she breathed his name again.

"Chase, I need directions to get you home."

Noticing her hand on his, his eyes took on a deeper hue. Electricity made a b-line to her abdomen, and she swore the butterflies multiplied. She couldn't move her hand away fast enough. If he looked at her another second that way she'd surely die from spontaneous combustion. A slow, devilish smile spread across his face, as if he knew. Her insides groaned.

Chase apparently resided just outside Portland. A gorgeous two-story house with light brown siding, chestnut colored shutters, and an attached garage that loomed at the end of a paved driveway. The house rested on an acre of private land with no other home in sight. She'd been living in a room so long this looked more like a mansion to her. Chase must have caught her gaping.

"Like what you see?"

Cassidy rubbed her arms against the early evening chill and approached him. From the sparkle in his captivating eyes she wondered whether he meant the house or himself. *He's referring to the house, idiot.*

"It's beautiful."

"Wait until you see inside."

After retrieving her bags and the groceries from the car she quickly caught up to him. Placing a hand gently at the small of her back, he ushered her toward the house. The warmth sent shivers coursing through her spine.

Inside the burden in her arms became too much, and she laid them down on the hardwood floor of the large, immaculate kitchen. Stove and refrigerator were chrome, counter tip and island were blue marble, and over the island hung a crystal chandelier reflecting specks of light against the walls like tiny stars. The kitchen table and chairs were a matching shade of blue. It looked modern, yet romantic. Her anxiety started to mount.

Chase led her to the living room down the hall. It looked like a page from a catalog with its massive wall-mount television, black leather sectional and matching recliner. A glass table sat in the center and a standing lamp loomed in two opposing corners. It seemed all the flooring in the house was hardwood.

At the back of the house, past a set of stairs leading upwards, was a sun-room with a wall length window overlooking a backyard pool, surrounded by apple trees. Inside the room, another black leather couch, computer, polished wooden desk and matching table, and a pricey looking stereo system. To her left, a glass door led to the backyard.

With all he possessed, materially, characteristically, he appeared superior to her. He'd always been smarter, better able to handle difficult people and problems, and knew how to speak to her, make her listen like nobody else. It seemed only he possessed a line straight to her heart, her psyche, and it scared her.

A brilliant man, possibly even gifted, winning academic awards while she struggled in school. She'd failed her first attempt at eleventh grade math while he was posted in the newspaper for earning medals for the same. Yet rather than be jealous, she'd been proud of him, and impressed at his humility since he never bragged.

A familiar sinking feeling, like so long ago, bubbled up. The urge to run overwhelmed her. Her lungs struggled to breathe, chest tightened painfully. He was better than her in a billion different ways. They were worlds apart. She knew the score, how it was, always would be. He was the sun, she was Icarus, and she'd never forget, and like Icarus, her destiny was to crash and burn.

She took a step back, her head bumping against his muscular chest. She couldn't stop trembling. *Suck it up Cassidy!* She prided herself on her ability to act with poise, but that all flew out the window in this crash course in reality. The warmth of his hand on her shoulder burned through the fabric, scorching her flesh.

"Is something wrong? You're shaking like a leaf."

She swallowed. "I'm fine."

Cassidy fought the burning in her eyes and squeezed her lids shut for a second as if that could stop a dam from bursting. She didn't dare look at him. She was anything but fine.

Chapter Four

Chase

Chase stared, bewildered. One minute she's impressed like she walked into Wonderland, the next she's got every wall up and is ready to bolt. She wasn't fine, at least not the way she insinuated. His arms ached to wrap around her but he feared it might driver her out the door, job loss or no. The rest of the tour had to wait. His jaw tensed. What would she do at the first sign of his stubborn streak?

"Want something to drink? I have beer."

He opted not to drink because of his medication, but once in a while he caved. His road to recovery was long, and he needed to unwind once in a while. Even without them, he drank little, preferring at least a measure of cognizance. Hyper-vigilance had become second nature after years of service, like a light being on and the off switch broken. At times, it exhausted him.

Cassidy walked past him, head lowered.

"Sure, sounds nice, thanks. Just let me get something from the car."

In silence he watched her go, his brain working overtime trying to figure out what happened. Something else he remembered, she brought a whole new level to the word confusion. With a rub of the slight scruff of his five o'clock shadow he went to the kitchen and grabbed a Moosehead from the fridge.

She came back much more composed. Without a word she put away the groceries with his guidance. He avoided getting too close, hoping to avoid a repeat of moments prior. When finished, he twisted off the cap and handed her the bottle.

"Thank you."

He nodded, nerves rattled as the situation dawned on him. Being alone, sleeping under the same roof as her, it was hard to ignore the feeling, both thrilling and terrifying, of wanting to do what he knew he shouldn't. She surely wouldn't allow him to. It was a challenge to overcome, and he always loved a challenge.

"You're welcome. I can show the rest of the house later. Want to listen to music?"

Music was always good for easing stress. Memories of her singing came to mind. She like to sing, had a beautiful voice, but at times tried to hard. Cassidy took a big gulp of her beer before answering.

"Sure."

They started back toward the sun-room.

"Anything you want to hear?" She shrugged.

"Whatever you want, I guess. I like all kinds."

Retrieving the laptop behind the stereo speakers he flipped it open, turned it on, then clicked the icon for the Chrome browser. In seconds he was on YouTube searching for music. After deciding on Aqua he sat by her on the couch, propping the cane to his side. It would still take a little while before his leg healed enough to lose it.

He'd been fortunate to survive, from what he heard. After his vehicle got hit, he narrowly escaped in one piece. The explosion sent him flying. Luckily, his comrades eliminated the threat, preventing further casualties. At least he'd heal and no major damage occurred to his body. That was the story relayed to him. He wished he could remember.

"Thank you." She muttered.

It was at the tip of his tongue to ask what she'd been up to the past few years when a vibration rumbled in her purse. Cassidy took out her phone, a slight pout formed on her face.

"Sorry, I have to get this."

She got up and stormed from the room. Might it be the same person who called earlier? He hated that look on her face, etched with such anxiety and fear. She had such a pretty smile...

A long stretch of silence ensued before her voice became audible.

"No Steve, we're done. It's been months, get over it."

Another stretch of silence.

"Well, you should have thought of that before you cheated on me, then hit me. Now stop calling. I want nothing more to do with you!"

Chase gaped. To eavesdrop was wrong, but instinct to protect flooded him. He wanted to figure out the problem and solve it. More silence.

"OK, I'm not telling you again. Stop bothering me or I'll call the cops. I got a restraining order for a reason!"

Chase straightened, chest tightening at the sound of her desperation. A restraining order? What trouble might this Steve be causing? A more primitive part of him wanted to punch the guy and he never even met him. If he set off mild-mannered Cassidy though, he more than likely deserved it.

He found himself tempted to inquire about the conversation but knew he shouldn't have been listening. He watched quietly as she sat back down and chugged back the rest of her drink.

"Would you like another?"

Cassidy's eyes reflected appreciation when she looked at him.

"No, thank you." That coy smile, so disarming. Were there any men who dared say 'no' to her?

The song finished and Crush by Garbage started. Must have found an automated playlist. Not one of his favorite songs, but he didn't want to move. She squirmed, then jump-started the conversation as though she couldn't start it fast enough.

"So what have you been up to?"

He told her of the places he'd been, where he lived while abroad, but never mentioned details of his missions. She seemed enthralled by his words, and commented on her interest in differing cultures, but most of the time she sat and listened. Many of their ideas and opinions on society and world events differed, but she was a smart woman.

They stayed up well into the night talking, reminiscing. More and more he realized how much he missed her. It felt like he was learning about her anew.

They both like video games, action movies, and chess, though he preferred comedy and played little chess. They even discussed favorite colors, but she refused to talk about her family. The things he most wanted to know she clung to with such a vice-like grip only the Jaws of Life could pry them from her. Perhaps it had been a qualifying factor that earned her the job.

He fought the onset of fatigue. A man of few words usually, he wanted to stay up just to watch those alluring lips move. It didn't hurt that her voice retained its youthful sound, unmistakably feminine, softer than cashmere, enough to harden a man. Combined with the way those clothes played off her figure, he couldn't help imagine what lay beneath them.

"I don't imagine you sleep upstairs at the moment, given your leg."

The sudden change of subject surprised him. It would have been too good to be true if she'd shared similar thoughts of him.

"No, I've been sleeping on the couch in the living room. I can show you upstairs now if you'd like."

She shook her head.

"No, I'll sleep on the couch in here. No sense making you aggravate your wounds when this is just as good." She patted the couch while stifling a yawn.

He straightened. He'd been so greedy, monopolizing her waking hours without though to what time she may have awoken or the strenuousness of her day.

"I should let you get some sleep."

She offered a coy grin.

"I'm alright. I just don't want you losing sleep for the sake of entertaining a guest."

He countered with a sly tilt at the corner of his lips.

"I'm not sure you qualify as one. But a lack of sleep might make you sloppy on the draw. Can't have that."

Cassidy glared daggers but said nothing. He wished he'd have known how fun it was to entice such fiery reactions from her. Try as he might, even armed head to toe, she didn't inspire fear. Cute was definitely one word on a list of many he'd use to describe her.

"The washroom is opposite the stairs if you need it. After a half hour I'd stay out of the living room, I sleep nude."

There was no hiding the shocked expression or crimson cheeks, no matter how fast she dashed for the bathroom. Her voice was barely perceptible as she closed the door behind her. Laughter was unavoidable, causing pain to slice through his ribs, leaving him clutching his side. He didn't care, it was worth it.

Chapter Five

Cassidy

Chase obviously said it to get under her skin and it worked. She hoped he hadn't seen how badly she blushed. Looking in the mirror, there was no denying her cheeks were beet red. *Get a hold of yourself, he was just yanking your chain!* Try as she might, there was no stopping her mind from wondering what Chase looked like in his birthday suit. *Jerk...*

Cassidy rushed to the kitchen to get her bags before returning to the washroom. Although a cold shower wouldn't hurt, exhaustion won out. She brushed, rinsed, changed into a black tank top and matching pants, and removed the elastic binding her hair. Silk strands cascaded just below her shoulders and she ran her fingers through the loose, gentle waves. Her weapons were the last to go in the bag for easy retrieval.

She held her breath, bidding her nerves to settle. Despite the pleasant conversation, she couldn't forget she was in way over her head. All she could do was hope for the best and prepared for the worst, even while so many questions rattled around her head.

Why didn't they just put him in some protection program, set him up in a residence at an undisclosed location, and let him see a licensed psychologist specializing in his situation? That would have been the normal thing to do, right? The more she reflected on it, the less it made sense. They may as well be dangling him like a worm on a hook, and she questioned the durability of the line. *Jim, what have you gotten me into?*

It made no sense for such an organization to waste money if they didn't find her to be of some use, but there were so many people more qualified that it seemed unfeasible. Might this be one big, sick joke? If so, it was definitely at her expense. It made her heart swell to see him again, but it wasn't the way she wanted.

She finished up and returned to the sun-room. Chase wasn't there, in his place rested a mauve comforter, neatly folded, and two pillows. It took effort to suppress the urge to go tell him not to push himself too much. If someone told her that while injured, she'd do it more. Not to mention what he said earlier. He may have been joking, but she didn't think herself ready to find out.

Within minutes she lay beneath the comforter, head nestled in downy pillows, staring at the ceiling in the dark. Her mind raced between thoughts of her mother, the whole situation she found herself in, not to mention how she was in Chase's house, sleeping on his couch. Everything seemed so crazy. Surely come morning, she would see this as having been nothing more than a strange dream.

Cassidy watched as Chase and three other people, all dressed in military attire, worked on assembling some computer like contraptions, things she didn't quite understand. He asked her to help and she couldn't tell him no. After a while it was time for bed. When she woke, she found she and his other comrades watching their replacements work.

She couldn't help the sense of inadequacy. He asked her what troubled her. When she replied he said he'd see her after the project's completion. She later waited outside an office similar to Mercer's, while Chase spoke to someone within. He came out, still in uniform. Upon seeing her, he smiled. One that left her pulse thrumming a quick staccato beat.

"Hi." She managed.

"Hey." the slow scan of his eyes as they raked the length of her body sent warm shivers through her spine.

Air caught in her lungs as those gorgeous blues focused on her, a devious grin on his face.

"Loose string." He pulled on it, somehow causing every button on her shirt to pop off.

Chase seemed undaunted by the fact someone might walk by any moment as he ran his hands up her bare stomach towards her aching breasts. Every nerve sizzled awake, and her legs became all the more aware of how her skirt floated just above her knees as moist tension centered between her thighs.

She leaned against the wall as the intensity washed over her when he found a hardened nub and teased. A breathy moan escaped her. He leaned in, his hot breath caressing her face, lips a hair-length away from hers...

Cassidy startled awake at the sound of her phone alarm. With a groan of frustration she reached in the bag by her head and shut it off. The dream was fresh in her mind and her body reeled from it. One thing she missed about home was the detachable shower head. She didn't trust her pocket rocket to be quiet enough. *It's waterproof you fool.* With any luck, the sound of the shower would drown out it out.

While nothing replaced genuine physical contact, she wasn't the one-nightstand kind of woman. She rummaged through her bag for the personal device. Better to deal with it under the circumstances. It was hazardous being so close to Chase, and she needed to keep distractions to a minimum. There was no telling what she'd gotten herself into, but with three lives on the line, lust was a more powerful obstacle to attention than she could afford to have.

At least it was a more pleasant dream than usual. Being chased by monsters and demons didn't make for good dreams at all. Considering the circumstances, she'd prefer the latter. Erotic dreams rarely occurred for her. Sometimes she wished it possible to avoid dreaming completely.

She brought what she needed to change and wash, then dealt with the issue at hand. After dressing, a knock on the door made her jump. Cassidy quickly wrapped her personal item in her overnight clothes and opened to see Chase donning just a pair of jeans, waving his free hand through the steam pouring from the bathroom.

Scars riddled his chiseled chest and torso, and her fingers barely resisted the urge to trace over them. Grateful didn't begin to describe the flurry of emotions at seeing him again, or having just released a lot of tension. If anything worse happened, she'd have regretted losing this opportunity. She forced her eyes away. She needed to escape. The sight of him left her wanting to do what she really shouldn't.

"Are you trying to set the bathroom on fire or is it always a sauna after you?"

Cassidy grabbed her things and rushed past him, unsure if that was sarcasm, or genuine displeasure.

"I like hot showers. Probably should have warned you, sorry."

"Glad I got a large tank."

Her cheeks flushed in embarrassment.

"I'll keep it lower from now on."

His laughter filled her ears.

"Don't worry. It doesn't bother me as long as there's some left for me."

She stopped, turned, smiled.

"Thank you."

"Oh, if you don't mind, I have physio this afternoon."

"Where and when?"

"Same place you got me, but on the first floor. Two o'clock."

She nodded, wondering if she'd be able to visit her mother without involving him. She was a private person about the hardships in her life. No denying she was an introvert. She'd need to be pretty comfortable with someone to open up, and social situations were taxing.

"It runs for about an hour and a half, two tops. The place is quite secure so you won't need to stay."

She tipped her head once more.

"Thanks."

Before she had the chance to ask if he needed anything, her phone rang. He walked in the bathroom as she pulled it from her pocket. She checked the caller ID. Jim. She had a few questions for him. Behind her she heard the door close, followed by the sound of running water.

"Hey Jim."

"Hey Cassy. How are things going with the assignment?" She didn't like being addressed by the shortened version of her name, but she'd always been too polite to say anything. There were worse things to worry about than that.

"Good, I guess. Not sure what's going on though. I think if it were me in charge, I'd put him in a special protection program, not in the hands of an amateur like myself. This whole thing is like baiting a hook and I feel like I'm being set up."

"You worry too much. In all the years I've known you, that's been an issue. There's a reason I chose you. You're resourceful and creative in a bind, quick, deceptively strong, persistent, and show a willingness to learn and learn fast. You certainly surpass all my expectations."

She suppressed a laugh, but didn't miss the fact he skirted the issue. Exactly how much did he know? She decided not to push and instead took it as extra incentive to keep on her toes.

"How'd I ever get a job for your company?"

"Very convincing references."

She imagined few people thought her capable of moving heavy furniture. Even having done that for years, until the company went out of business, no other company dared hire her. She could only imagine why.

Then came Jim. He saw her strength, and took it upon himself to be her mentor, took a chance on her, trained her, even guided her to the people who taught her how to fight and shoot. He found a broken vessel and helped patch it back together. Jim was irreplaceable.

"Yeah, my friends could sell ice to a penguin." She chuckled, as did he.

"No doubt. Anyway, I have other projects to set up, just wanted to check in. Keep focused and depending on how things go, we may have something to discuss."

His words surprised her. *No pressure there...*

"Sure thing, Jim. I'll do my best."

"Always." With that, he hung up.

Never before did Jim remind her to do her job. He must have been feeling immense pressure. What was her role in this whole thing? The weight of the world crashed on her shoulders. She understood then that something going wrong wasn't a matter of if, but when.

In seconds she was on the line with Marc.

"Cassidy, we missed you last night! Something wrong?"

Even though she trusted him, she took confidentiality seriously.

"No, no. Everything's fine. Jim just has me on a special assignment right now and I only found out last minute. I can't say much. Confidentiality, you know."

"Special assignment? Is it a Messiah Prophet concert?" She smiled.

Marc was nice guy, reliable type. A shoulder to lean on if needed. He was there for her the night she found out about her mother's accident and showed amazing support. He also wasn't afraid to throw a punch if necessary, like the last time her ex showed up and tried to lay a hand on her.

Marc was on him in the blink of an eye. She held zero tolerance for abusive behavior and immediately put a stop to the relationship, planned to anyway because of the cheating. Unfortunately, she didn't pick up on his abusive tendencies before it was too late, and his stalker qualities became apparent.

"Sorry, no. It's not a concert at all, but that's all I can tell you. Well, that, and I'll be sleeping somewhere else for a while because of it."

"You can still do poker night, right?"

She didn't know how to work that. It wasn't that she was embarrassed by her friends, but by her financial situation. Lately poker night involved Smarties and what movie to play on movie night instead of cash. Maybe that was a bit square, she didn't care.

The most exciting thing she did was play RockBand. So what if she sounded worse than Alanis Morissette? That didn't stop her from doing what she enjoyed.

She'd endured enough ridicule in life for not fitting in and didn't need to give Chase a reason to do so. She needed to remember, it was just a mission, a job. Once finished, no doubt he'd want to go on his merry way and not deal with her again.

"Not sure. I'd love to try. It would suck missing poker night." *And RockBand...*

"Yeah, it would. Don't worry about calling Stacy, I'll let her know."

Stacy was a true friend whose coping mechanism was shopping. During the worst of times, chocolate. Both her and Marc made great sparring partners during workouts, which she'd done at home for the last few weeks because of her financial difficulties.

Second hand videos and YouTube lists and subscriptions had become a God send. Even though she didn't get the same level of in-depth training as she would from a personal trainer, she didn't stop at one fighting style either. It would do for the time being, but she couldn't wait to get back on track.

Stacy being a dark-haired bombshell didn't affect their friendship at all. They'd known each other since elementary school. Even though Stacy moved to Russia because of her parents, they'd kept in touch. At twenty-three, Stacy returned, and they'd been roommates and best friends ever since.

"OK."

The bathroom door opened.

"Sorry, but I have to go. Talk to you guys later."

"Yep. Be safe. Later."

Cassidy had the phone in her pocket before Chase walked in, water glistening off his torso.

Cassidy swallowed, turned her head. No, no, no. Her earlier efforts would not be for naught. Why couldn't he have at least worn a shirt? She hoped he wouldn't expect her to help him bathe and dress. If she had to she would, but the idea made her extremely uncomfortable.

She bit her lip, placing her weapons on her person, fighting the urge to scan him. For all she knew, he turned into a complete jerk. Whatever helped her focus, even if it felt like she was lying to herself.

He leaned against the wall, watching her. She suppressed a shiver. He wouldn't make this easy. His voice was like warm honey to her ears.

"So, what would you be doing today, if you weren't stuck with me?"

She peered at him. Big mistake. With arms crossed as he leaned against the wall, injured leg resting over his good one, he cut a majestic figure. His scars detracted nothing from his charm. Blue eyes ignited with mischief. Forcing hers away, she replaced items in her bag and tucked it beside the couch.

"Covering for someone on vacation. This was last minute notice."

The corner of his lip twitched upward, giving a look capable of tempting a girl to sin. She was no longer that girl.

"No plans with friends? A boyfriend?"

"No, and no. You?"

His eyes became sullen, and she sensed his nervous energy. Instinctively, she changed the subject. At least the idea of him having a girlfriend helped enforce the 'hands off' thing.

"Anything I need to know about your recovery regimen?"

"Before you, I had hired help, but they wanted an arm and a leg, and the Sergeant was hoping for a 'jack of all trades'."

Of course. She shouldn't complain, at least it was going to her, and her mother direly needed any extra she attained.

"I guess I can understand. Have you had breakfast? I suppose I should get right to it."

He uncrossed his arms, straightened, took hold of his cane.

"I had cereal so I'm not hungry. Usually have that in the mornings, but lunch and supper you can help with. Also, housekeeping." She nodded.

"Alright. I'll get started, just have a couple more calls to make."

He looked like he had another quip in mind but kept it to himself.

"Excuse me." She brushed past him and left the room. Last thing she wanted was him knowing anything about her mother. She still had to call the Sergeant Major as well.

To open up is to give someone the ability to hurt you. That's why she found it so important to be wary of what she said, and to whom. Regardless of what she thought of him years ago, he may be a different person. A teenage girl can be naïve, and she supposed she was. Even then, she had the sense not to talk about her problems. When it came to that, she'd rarely been a fool.

Chapter Six

Chase

He was unsure how to respond when asked whether he had a girlfriend. The woman he'd been with for years one day took off. It was infuriating to the point of overriding any hurt it should have caused, not just because she left, but how and why, and right before deployment. There were a few choice words rolling in his head to describe her, none good. No way she hadn't been cheating. He shook the thoughts from his head. No need to dwell on the negative.

His eyes had a mind of their own as they drank in the view of her curves and backside as she left. The hair matted to her back tempted him to touch, and he wondered if she hid a wild side. She was so secretive he bet getting to know her more intimately would be like peeling an onion. He gritted his teeth.

What did it matter? She'd take off in the end. Drop off the face of the earth like last time. He'd missed her, but she remained a flight risk.

For far too long he stared at the ceiling the night before, thinking about the situation, her, their past, before sleep claimed him. Memories surfaced, long forgotten, things she did, said. One memory in particular made him wonder about her character, behavior, something that might explain one of the many reasons she felt the need to distance herself from him so thoroughly.

Vibrations in his back pocket brought him to the here and now. He retrieved his cell. Aiden. A fellow man-in-arms. The guy was an oddball, his antics good for a laugh when an increase in morale was necessary. God knew he needed a distraction.

"Hey!"

"Mind if I stop by? Just got Diablo III, didn't realize my sis got me the game for my birthday. Thought you'd like to have it."

He smiled.

"Sure, but I have physio at two."

"Understood. See you soon."

Aiden was more of a drinker than he, and much more flirtatious. Since Cassidy wasn't the type, there would surely be some entertainment. A grin played on his lips. Perhaps he was mildly sadistic.

He made his way upstairs, hissing from the shooting pain ripping through his leg like wild fire. The effort sped his breathing and caused his side to ache. He didn't understand his sense of urgency to cover his body. Perhaps the way Cassidy continuously avoided looking at his chest bothered him more than it should have. It was his home, he could do as he pleased in any state of dress, but for whatever reason, he just couldn't.

Her voice traveled through the vents, hushed yet distressed. Despite his better judgment he inclined his ears toward the sound until he reached his room, unable to pick out more than a couple of words. Standing over his polished mahogany dresser, he leaned forward, browsing the shirts. In a flash his leg kinked out and a rush of pain flooded him. He collapsed with an agonized roar.

Breaking out in a sweat, he reached for his cane. Embarrassment burned in his veins. He didn't care if Cassidy's job required her to help, he didn't want her to, didn't want help from anyone. All he wanted was everything back to normal. Rage at his shortcomings spread like flames within. Helplessness was intolerable.

Creaking stairs announced her impending arrival as his trembling arms lacked the strength to support his efforts. He collapsed once more, leg throbbing, once again awash in pain upon landing. Her hand hovered over her weapon as she quickly scanned the room before setting her eyes on him.

With a sigh she approached, halting at his glaring warning. Her concerned expression intensified. He waved a hand in dismissal.

"I can do this." He rasped.

Uncertainty radiated from her but she waited as he tried two, three more times without success, yet he managed to slide onto his bed. If she rolled her eyes, he never noticed. Sweat pooled beneath him, soaking his sheets. The wheels in her head turned, but she said nothing, only scanned the room before her focus fell on the open dresser drawer.

The tongue lashing he expected, that he usually received from doctors, therapists, friends, and family about his stubborn streak didn't come. Instead, she rummaged thoughtfully through his drawer before picking up a grey shirt and toying with it. Where was the girl that yelled at him for playing in traffic? The woman that stood before him seemed far more careful with her words.

"Maybe you want a bath before you dress. I'll bring clothes down so you don't have to keep coming up here."

A bath would be great, even though he already had one. He got the impression she was giving him an out. Who was he to refuse? Even though he didn't like people going through his things, he was too drained to argue.

"Yeah, sounds fine." The idea of going down stairs at that moment filled him with dread.

Ignoring the pain in his chest he forced himself to sit.

"Are you able to stand?"

With effort he managed, barely. Her eyes scanned him as she dropped the shirt back in the drawer. Another assessment of him from head to toe, he swallowed. What was she doing? Many ideas raced through his head and the room suddenly felt about twenty degrees hotter. So she probably wasn't the type to do the things he had in mind, a man could dream.

He stiffened as she came to about an inch from him. One more scan, she turned, pressed tight against him, and lifted him up. She encircled her arms behind his legs, wrapped them around her waist, and lifted. He threw his arms around her delicate shoulders to keep from falling over. It amazed him how quickly she steadied herself and straightened. Shock overcame him.

"What the hell is wrong with you? I'm a grown man! You'll kill yourself on those stairs!" In the midst of his surprise he forgot his cane.

"It's fine, really. I've done this before." Strain was vaguely apparent in her tone.

He held his tongue from asking. What a piss off and a shame. At least none of his buddies were there, he'd never hear the end of it. Had she always been so strong?

Her soft, silken skin and floral scent teased him. Feather light strands caressed his cheek. His body's traitorous reaction was a slap to the face of his ego.

Not until he reached the edge of the tub did he release the breath he'd been holding. As she rose, he got a wonderful up close view of her derriere. At such proximity it was obvious she worked out. She stepped away and turned.

Her face expressed relief. Beads of sweat glistened along the sides of her face as her cheeks burned a lovely shade of pink. With a finger, she brushed the hair over her shoulder, away from her face, and his eyes fell to her chest. Standing before him, she painted a picture of pure femininity that belied the fact she'd just hauled his ass down the stairs like a worker mule. Inwardly he groaned.

She fidgeted nervously.

"I'll be right back with some clothes and a towel."

In silence he watched her hustle out. After what just happened, he refused to ask her help. So his stubbornness was a contributing factor to the other help leaving. He wondered how they'd have fared in his shoes. Being reliant on others for the simplest tasks was no way to live. He may have improved, but still had some healing left to do, and being carted around like a helpless child was incredibly demeaning.

Upon returning she hung his clothes and towel on the wall-rack and handed him a face cloth before leaning his cane against the wall.

"Do you need any help?"

Perhaps it was the blow to his pride, but he lost all patience.

"No, I can manage."

"You sure? Need anything else?"

He stared her down.

"What do you want? Praise for the amazing feat of carrying me down the stairs, or are you hoping for a look at the goods?"

Her eyes widened, horrified, and she stepped back, face burning crimson.

"No! I'm just trying to..."

"I don't need anymore of your help. Get out!"

At first she looked about to cry, but her eyes just as quickly stared shards of ice. In spite of himself he found her ferocity arousing.

"As you wish, *Agent Averey*."

Warnings rang through his head. Cassidy was more than just a hired help and if he didn't keep his pride in check, he'd lose her all over again. After starting the bath he flung off his jeans and boxers before sliding into steaming water. The heat soothed his muscles, he sank deeper.

Maybe he overreacted a little. He didn't want to worry about it when company was coming. There was enough to think about. At least he'd known Aiden for years. The guy may be wacky, but no traitor.

Once the water cooled he cleaned quickly, ignoring the discomfort of his ribs and leg. Dried, clothed, he grabbed his cane and headed for the living room. To his surprise his three-drawer nightstand sat beside the couch, its contents now resting on top. He watched her slide a box of bedding beneath the couch.

"What's this? You're rearranging my furniture?" He rubbed the top of his head, confused.

Wasn't she just bringing some apparel down, not converting his living room into another bedroom? She stood, smirked.

"Thought this would be easier for you. Better to limit your trips upstairs until your leg is better." Cassidy straightened.

"Why? You could have just brought a bag down instead."

She shrugged.

"Just trying to do my job."

The inflection in her words made him cringe. Perhaps he had been too harsh with her, but he didn't see a reason to apologize. It wasn't like he'd hurt her. Besides, she'd pushed it but messing with his masculinity. Doubtful she even understood the significance. After a brief moment deliberating what he should say, the doorbell rang. Hesitantly, he answered.

"Hey man!" Aiden gave a quick pat on the back as he showed the game, still wrapped.

"You!" Her voice came out a terse whisper and Aiden backed away, eyes on her.

Alarms went off in his head like the fourth of July. Aiden looked stunned.

"Do I know you?"

She crossed her arms, expression furious.

"What a stupid question from someone who tried to run a pregnant woman over with a car!"

Chase straightened. No way. Aden may have an odd sense of humor, but it didn't border on the morbid.

"Are you sure it was him?" Her eyes cut him down.

"I was there..." Aiden laughed nervously.

"I wasn't really trying to, it was a joke."

"Even making a joke of running a pregnant woman over is NOT funny! If you can't be trusted with the safety of one vulnerable civilian, how can anyone trust you to help defend a country? It's unfathomable and sickens me that even one *penny* of my tax dollars might contribute to your salary!"

He'd never seen Cassidy like this before. As heated as wildfire with as much bite as a bullet.

"Cassidy!"

Her eyes fell on him and despite their ferocity, not an ounce of fear trickled in his veins. It only made him wonder at the possibility of igniting that fire in other ways.

"Don't tell me you'd defend what he did."

"No, I..."

"It was a joke, nobody got hurt. No need to be such a bitch about it."

"You're an idiot. I'd rearrange your face but I wouldn't want your blood on me."

Chase's eyes widened. This was not the Cassidy he remembered. He understood feeling that way, assuming it was true, but he didn't think Aiden would have done anything. A stupid move nonetheless. Aiden laughed.

"Scared of a little blood?"

Cassidy laughed in return.

"Nope, scared of a little herpes. Yeah, I know about that. That's what you get for being so reckless. I suppose after what you did, some might call it karma."

Aiden advanced, ready to pounce on her, but Chase intervened.

"Let's go out back and try that game. I've been itching to for ages."

It took a second but his words sank in.

"Yeah, just keep *it* out here."

Cassidy merely stared after them, arms crossed, as they left the room. They discussed the game while playing but his mind couldn't leave the incident. Had he underestimated her? She'd always come across as a passive person. He'd do well to remember Mercer hired her for a reason, especially knowing the extent of his stubborn nature.

"So, what's with the broad?"

The sudden question surprised him. As much as he wanted to tell him, an order was an order, and there was no telling about the other people Aiden associated with. What had Mercer said about painting a domestic picture?

"She's my girlfriend."

Aiden leaned back, stunned.

"Bullshit! How come I never heard about this?"

"It's only been a short time, but she offered to help out after learning I had none."

Aiden laughed.

"You mean she doesn't know your pissy attitude scared them off?"

She's probably figuring that out now...

"No, she doesn't."

Aiden leaned forward, facing the monitor, stifling a chuckle.

"I think it'll be funny to see who scares who off first. She's a real spitfire."

He shook his head in disbelief at the heated exchange between the two.

"It would seem."

Chapter Seven

Cassidy

If she were the type of person to judge others based on the company kept instead of their own actions, she'd have determined that Chase had become a complete idiot, and an ass. His flipping out when she only tried to do her job cleared things up big time. This thing with Aiden, even more so. She'd heard that when people join the forces, they never came back the same.

The man she worked with delivering furniture came to mind. He'd suffered a head injury during a training exercise after jumping from a helicopter and was apparently never the same. Failed parachute. His PTSD, or whatever he had flared up bad, and he had flashbacks. It got too much for him and he quit, disappeared. She missed working with him and hoped he was doing better. He'd always been kind to her.

Things like that sent painful jabs to the back of her head because it stirred up thoughts of Chase. She vehemently fought them because she'd worry and they'd lost touch since he'd left the country on his last tour of duty, never informing her of his return. It stung deep. She shook her head.

Here and now, she had a job. One that would hopefully provide the finances required to cover her mother's care. She should be grateful for Chase's outburst, it gave her clarity to focus. At the end, he'd be eager for her departure. At least she wouldn't have to deal with Aiden afterwards.

He deserved that tongue lashing, doubtful he'd learned anything. She could see him as the type to sleep around without due care, not taking responsibility for his actions. It terrified her that people like that existed. Aiden wasn't trustworthy, end of story.

She refused to think about them anymore, instead focusing on cleaning. She nearly smashed her phone when Steve's number popped up again. Guys like him were the reason for restraining orders. How unfortunate a piece of paper lacked the ability to stop him from bothering her. Otherwise, it would actually prove useful.

An hour before noon, she started on lunch. By noon, the mouthwatering scent of spiced chicken and rice with broccoli and onions had her stomach rumbling. As she set two full dishes on the table, the men entered. Cassidy suppressed a frown. She *really* didn't want to eat with Aiden.

"What smells so good?" Chase inspected the food on his plate.

"Chicken and rice. Nothing fancy."

The men sat and ate. She watched a moment as they scarfed down their food. Did they remember how to breathe? She'd had many compliments for her cooking, but never quite like this. She hoped they didn't choke.

"Wow! They should serve this while abroad instead of those disgusting MRE's."

She looked at Aiden quizzically. What the hell was an M-R-E? Chase seemed to sense her question.

"Meals Ready-to-Eat. Nicer way of saying rations."

"Oh..." She had no idea what they ate, but assumed Chicken-a-la-King wasn't part of the menu. Aiden swallowed a bite and laughed.

"That shit's disgusting. The best thing is the crackers and peanut butter. Everything else tastes like cardboard. Unless you're lucky enough to get a packet of Tabasco sauce. I'd rather just eat that."

"Sounds horrible!" An understatement. They deserved better than that. Chase shifted uncomfortably.

"You going to sit and eat?" Chase took another bite.

She grabbed her own plate and sat, moving further from Chase.

Sitting beside him was to uncomfortable an idea. Aiden held his fork as he stared at her. Chase didn't seem to notice. If he did, he didn't let on. Aiden was too attentive for her liking.

"For a couple, you sure don't act like it."

Chase told him they were together? She thought that was only for the outside world, not those closest to Chase who knew him best. Then again, she had no clue how close they were, how long they'd been friends. Really, she was clueless about everything.

A younger Cassidy would do back-flips and somersaults at the idea. At least, on the inside. When you can't have a clean conversation with a guy on the phone without being called a whore by a heavy-handed father, you learn to keep your mouth shut, and hands to yourself. That wasn't touching on her mother freaking about the clothes she wore as if they were visible to the person on the other end. Yeah, her childhood was messed up.

Older, wiser Cassidy didn't want to stoke the fires. If there was anything left of teenage Cassidy, she'd have buried her. Already she felt crazy for having something for someone who would never return her affections. If only she were able to just turn it off like a light switch, then pull out all the wires.

She forced a smile to hide her surprise as Chase spared her a glance.

"Chase has been on edge lately, so I try to give him some space. God knows he can get pretty crabby when he knows he needs help."

Aiden's chest rumbled from laughter as he dropped his fork on his plate. If he hated her, it seemed forgotten for the moment. It didn't make her distrust him any less.

"Isn't that the truth? I'm sure you'd love to chat with all his former help. They definitely..."

"Cassidy..."

If looks could kill, Aiden would have died a hundred times over. Aiden sensed it too and resumed eating. Chase offered his most devilish smile, mischief pouring from his eyes, like he either wanted to kiss her or kill her. She bet on the latter.

"Why not move closer? No need to be timid. I'm just stressed, that's all."

Hesitantly she did as requested. Other women might have rushed at his beckon for that gleam in his eye, but not her. Still, there was no denying the crook of his lip left a warmth flooding to the center of her hips. *You're so hopeless...* She started on her meal.

It didn't take a genius to guess what Aiden meant to say. She'd caught a glimpse of Chase's stubborn nature and could only imagine the extent. It was only a matter of time before she found out. The important thing to remember was she did this for her mother. It shouldn't have astonished her he hadn't been entirely honest about the departure of the previous help. Honesty was important to her.

He wrapped an arm around her, leaned in, and placed a light kiss on her temple. Quick, simple, but left a tingling sensation behind.

"Let's catch a movie later. We can rent one from Cineplex." Her body melted beneath his sweltering gaze.

"Sure. Sounds great."

Chase examined her thoroughly, focusing on her chest before reaching her eyes with a look that could melt steel.

"You look nice today. Is that a new shirt?"

He had to be putting on a show. He sounded so convincing, but she knew better. Should it bother her so much that he lied so well? It frightened her to think he might find it so easy. *It's all an act! You're supposed to be acting!* Try as she might, her feelings weren't fake.

He leaned in, traced a finger along the length of her neck, sending an ache to her chest. While her body craved his touch, her inclination toward self-preservation screamed for her to run.

She reminded herself this was all for her mother. Chase didn't make this easy. Especially when he whispered in her ear, just loud enough for Aiden to hear.

"With any luck, I'll see you without it later."

While only a show, her body didn't care. It was in full rebellion against her brain. There was no stopping the tremor coursing through her. From Aiden's expression, he definitely heard. She tried for an even tone.

"I bet you have your way with all the ladies." She gave a playful slap to his arm and chuckled. Inside she didn't doubt. She'd seen him flirt and had no desire to be a notch in someone's belt. For her, it was all or nothing.

"I think I should go before you guys defile the table." Aiden stood, his attention fell to her.

"I suppose I should thank you for not poisoning my meal." Now that was the expected reaction. Humor was apparent in her voice.

"Sorry to disappoint, maybe next time." He nodded.

She wouldn't really do it unless lives depended on it. She ignored Chase's bewildered expression.

"Fair enough." Aiden started toward the door. "Later, Chase." He waved on his way out.

Awkward silence ensued. She moved to the other side of the table. Another second beside him would result in the fire department cleaning her ashes off the ceiling. So much for her earlier efforts.

"You two know each other?"

She shook her head.

"Not really. The only time I saw him was when he attempted vehicular homicide. Other than that, it's the six degrees of separation. A friend of a friend." She resumed eating, avoiding his questioning gaze.

"You two ever..."

Why even ask? She saw a chance to toy with him. Serve him right after messing with her insides. It's the least he deserved. She set down her fork.

"What, you mean before or after the herpes?"

His eyes widened for a split-second and she found it impossible to suppress a laugh.

"No, we never did anything."

He eyed her with scrutiny. What was he thinking? She sensed his negative energy and her discomfort grew.

"I was messing with you. Never did anything with him. I'm not a one-night-stand kind of person. More of a long-term, marriage sort of deal."

His face became stoic. She squirmed. Had she said something wrong? Why ask a question when the answer may displease? Why care in the first place? Chalking it up to nothing more than curiosity she changed the subject. There was no other reason for him to ask and she refused to reflect on it anymore. Getting away from the situation became her main priority.

"I'll just finish up here. You can do something else if you want."

He opened his mouth to speak.

"Your physio is soon and there are things I have to do before I take you." *Like scrub the house from top to bottom until I'm too exhausted to think or feel.*

He sighed.

"I never meant to make you uncomfortable, but we can't take chances when someone's corresponding with the enemy. Even a friend can get dragged into it and be forced to speak under duress. It's important to leave nothing for the opposition to work with. Nothing can be left to chance." She released a breath.

"I get it. Mercer made it pretty clear. Everything's an act, I realize that. It just surprised me. I figured you and Aiden were good friends. I'll do better."

"Don't worry so much. I understand he chose you for a reason. You probably just need to warm up to the task. Just remember, there's much on the line and we can't afford mistakes."

That frightened her. Mistakes were unavoidable, at least when it came to her personal life. Disaster to her was like flames to gasoline. A frown spread across her face and she nodded.

"Got it."

Chase stood, retrieved a bottle of water from the refrigerator and swallowed a pill from a container in his pocket. On his way out he turned.

"You're welcome to watch TV with me when you're done."

She smiled.

"Thank you."

Turned out she had no time. Too much housework. At least that was her excuse. In reality the tension was overwhelming. Too much going on, too much weight on her shoulders.

Relief washed over her as they made their way to the therapy room of the heavily secured building. A well built man with short charcoal hair and intelligent chocolate eyes greeted them, bearing the resemblance and garb of an employee.

"Agent Averey, so glad you made it!" They shook hands.

"You can go now, Cassidy. I'm fine here for the next couple of hours."

She scanned the room, eyeing the equipment curiously, unable to name most of them.

"I'll come back later, then." She waved goodbye and left.

The drive to the hospital was a blur. So many things clouded her mind, questions with no answers, fear with no assuagement. Nothing made sense. Her feelings, the job, what Mercer told her, all of it a jumbled mess in her head. She couldn't see being anything more than a stand in since she lacked any of the skills and training found in the army. Marc and Stacy warned her about her potential to be over-analytical. Perhaps they were right, but that didn't make her wrong.

Before long she parked in the underground lot of the hospital, made unsteady strides toward her mother's room on the fourth floor, and forced a slow breath. Her heart beat so wildly she feared it would leap from her chest. Seeing the poor woman on all those life support machines broke her heart every time. Body trembling, she pressed her lips to her mother's slightly creased forehead.

Catherine, a beautiful woman in her mid fifty's, appeared peaceful. Cassidy received most of her looks from her, just not the better features. Catherine's nose was finer, more aquiline, and her eyes were like deep green marble. When her mother smiled people gravitated to her. She possessed a natural charisma Cassidy found impossible to emulate.

It was a while before she spoke as she gazed upon her mother, enveloped in the sterile atmosphere of white, aside from the constantly beeping machines. At one point she found it annoying, but learned to appreciate them. Somewhere along the line they came to mean life, and she couldn't put a price on that, though apparently the doctor could.

The bed depressed slightly as she sat at the edge. People have said a person in a coma can sometimes hear what goes on around them, even if they can't acknowledge anything. She didn't know, but wouldn't discount the possibility.

"Hi mom. I hope they're treating you well." she rubbed her mother's arm, avoiding the tubes and protruding needles.

Still no acknowledgment. The expected response, just not the one she wanted. A moment of silence.

"My boss gave me another assignment. I can't tell you what it is, but it's different than usual." Another bout of silence.

She squeezed her mothers' hand.

"It's supposed to pay better so I'm hoping it will help with medical expenses. If so, they can hopefully do more, and you can get better faster." It was a struggle to keep the floodgates closed when all she wanted to do was cry. At least it was a private room.

"Miss Macayla?"

She spun quickly, heart racing. Her mind had been so preoccupied she never heard the doctor enter. The middle-aged man ran a hand through his salt-and-pepper hair, hazel eyes stern, expression guarded.

"Sorry to startle you. Please, come with me. We have something to discuss."

Bile rose in her throat as she stood, nodded. From his posture she figured this would be bad.

"Of course." They proceeded to an office near the end of the brightly lit hallway.

Once seated before his wooden desk, she eyed him intently, waiting impatiently for him to speak. Finally she asked.

"What's going on?"

He considered his words before replying.

"As you know, we've been monitoring your mother closely, and have picked up on a developing problem, likely caused by the trauma to her head."

Cassidy's mouth went dry. *Oh no...*

"What is it?"

"Your mother has developed a cerebral aneurysm. It's been growing steadily, and while we hoped it would stop, it hasn't. She needs an operation."

The news was a punch to the gut, her heart sank to the floor. How would this affect her mother? Would she recover?

"We believe the best course of action is an occlusion and bypass." Her brows scrunched in confusion.

"What's that?"

"That's when we clamp off the artery leading to the aneurysm and attach a small blood vessel to the artery to reroute the blood away from the damaged area. For the surgery we'll use anesthesia as we would under normal circumstances."

She wrung her hands nervously. The concept of brain surgery terrified her.

"Will she be OK?"

The doctor folded his hands over his desk, entwining his fingers.

"There are risks associated with any surgery. Unfortunately, it's gotten to the point we believe it will rupture, and cause further brain damage, possibly even death. Risks of surgery include infection, damage to surrounding tissue, bleeding, and seizures, but if nothing gets done, her chances of survival or almost nil."

A piece of her wanted to die. No way, this wasn't happening.

"Can it kill her?"

His lips pursed tightly.

"It's a possibility, but her condition has reached a point where if surgery is not performed, it will rupture, and death has the highest probability of occurring."

Dread consumed her. So either the aneurysm could kill her, or the surgery. Childhood memories of camping trips and long Sunday drives raced through her mind. She wanted to dig up the drunk driver so she could kick him, over and over, until there was nothing left but an unrecognizable heap.

"Now the surgery will take about four hours, and we'll administer her medication intravenously."

"Can you show me this aneurysm?"

He pulled a file from his desk and retrieved a dark, transparent page with a picture of her mothers' brain. The aneurysm was clearly visible, but he pointed it out anyway. She swallowed against the cotton feeling in her mouth. For the first time she wished her father was still alive. He could be making all these tough decisions. Despite what he'd done to her, them, surely he'd have been useful for something.

Losing her father was more of a relief. He certainly wouldn't have won father of the year. But losing her mother would be devastating. Fear and pain welled up.

"If this is her best hope, then do what you have to do."

He put the page back in the file and replaced it in the drawer.

"There's something else you may need to consider."

It didn't take a genius to know what was coming. It wasn't an option, couldn't be. They'd been through this months ago. She didn't dare. Miracles happened daily. Catherine could wake any time.

"I'm not having her disconnected. It's not happening." She put as much firmness in her tone as possible.

"I understand your position, but after a while the chances of her coming out of this diminish significantly. If this doesn't work, we may have no other choice."

"It will. It has to." She folded her arms defiantly.

How dare he presume to understand how she felt? He pulled a form from another drawer.

"We can discuss this at a later time. For now, you must sign this so we can proceed."

She scribbled her name quickly after skimming through, then slid it toward him. It was a consent form explaining the procedure and medication.

"How soon can you operate?"

"Two weeks." Full panic mode set in, but she fought it, fiercely.

"Can't you do it sooner?" He shook his head.

"Sorry, unless there's a cancellation, that's the soonest. Usually the wait time is a month, minimum."

That seemed so unfair. She fidgeted in her seat.

"This is ridiculous. If it's so dangerous, I'd think you'd want to rush this."

"I assure you, we'll deal with it as soon as we can." She stood.

"Thank you, doctor."

"You're welcome, Miss Macayla."

Thanking him was the last thing she wanted to do. She wanted to scream, throw things, have a tantrum like a two-year-old. Instead she shook his hand.

"I'll go back and check on her."

With a nod she left. It was just her luck when things went wrong, they went very wrong. Her cell rang on the way to her mothers' room. Pulling it from her pocket she cursed as Steve's name popped up on the screen. A blip followed, indicating an incoming message. Her blood chilled.

We need to talk and since you won't answer my calls, I'll have to find you. You need to know I never meant to hurt you, and I'll do whatever it takes for you to listen. I'm not giving up.

Threatening to involve the police didn't work. A restraining order didn't work. This guy was about fifty cards short of a full deck. If he didn't lay off, it could affect her job. Something told her that would be the least of her problems. Every instinct screamed things were about to get much worse.

Chapter Eight

Chase

Sweat drenched his skin head to toe. The grueling session had finally finished, and he sighed in relief.

"You did a great job today. You've improved significantly, better than expected." Carter, his therapist, patted him on the back.

"Thanks! Nothing personal, but when do we stop meeting like this?" Carter chuckled.

He never regretted joining the forces, but it wasn't all fun and games. His reasons for joining had nothing to do with parental influence, especially since his father was absent most of his life. He merely wanted to make a difference for the better.

There was also the excitement of being in the field. Normal sometimes seemed boring after you've had to run for your life so many times. Once his health returned, he'd go back, if permitted. Adrenaline was like a drug. Who'd have thought?

The injury to his brain concerned him most. He didn't want to consider termination if his seizures were lifelong. Wasn't supposed to be, only until he regained his memory, but there's always that chance. He'd only had a couple so far and needed something more to jog his memory. They'd tried everything but live action. If that's what it took, so be it.

"That's up to the Sarge, but considering your progress, I'd wager not much longer."

Chase stood, making his way to the locker rooms in the back. A few minutes remained before Cassidy showed up, and the need for a shower was dire. What he most wanted was a nap, and to play more on the computer. These sessions were exhilarating as well as draining.

"Can't wait."

His mind wandered as his muscles relaxed beneath a cascade of hot water as he scrubbed on his favorite body wash. He had to admit that perhaps hiring Cassidy was a mistake. Not only did it bother him to think he might lose her in an obvious trap, he questioned her suitability for the job. It took more than knowledge on how to shoot or fight to get a job done.

What could she possibly know about military tactics? Things that took years to master, and what the traitor used. He would not be left alone, and she doubtfully contained the foresight to keep her eyes open to danger of this magnitude. Being incapacitated weighed heavily. While he tried to shrug it off, it didn't come easily.

To remain focused was key. Keeping control and a clear mind meant the difference between life and death. He found himself unable to shake the notion that his enemy, like a vulture, circled for the kill. Question remained, how long before the strike?

Once dry, he played through the pain of dressing, then went to the entrance where Cassidy waited. He froze. Her eyes were red, swollen, like she'd been crying, yet she pasted on a smile when she saw him. There was no hiding it, something was wrong.

"You ready to go?" A tremor sifted through her voice.

He wanted to help, to fix the problem. What made her so upset? The sight tore up his insides. Was it the guy she spoke to before?

"You alright?" He shouldn't care, especially after what happened with his ex. Lesson learned, don't trust women when you work in a profession that takes you away for months at a time. Cassidy seemed different. She snapped straight.

"What? I'm fine. Is there anywhere you need to stop before heading home?"

As tight-lipped as ever. Why did she have such difficulty opening up to him? It wasn't so bad years ago when she spoke to him in private that day. What happened since then?

Did she also remember? Had she meant it? Why did he still care? He figured these questions would plague him for the rest of his life. Her unrelenting hold to secrecy gnawed at him.

"No, let's head back. I want to play Diablo." She tilted her chin slightly.

"Alright."

They made way to her car in silence, the drive fared no better. The urge to say something, to break the awkward silence, eroded his insides. He wanted to lift her mood, but she didn't always react like other women. Trying to figure her out was a challenge. Stricken blasted through the speakers and she turned the volume down slightly.

"Have you played that before?"

She gave a sideways glance, brow raised as if perplexed by his audacity in speaking.

"No, I don't play PC games. I prefer XBox and Playstation."

He never pegged her as a gamer, more a dancer.

"What games do you enjoy?"

She smiled.

"Lots of things. Resident Evil, though the newer ones piss me off. The bosses are insane. Lots of zombie related things. Then there's Final Fantasy eight and ten. Umm... Almost anything Elder Scrolls related, like Skyrim and Elder Scrolls online. Fear Two, most anything psychological and scary."

He couldn't see getting into the zombie thing, but he'd played the PC version of Elder Scrolls online. It was difficult, so many bugs. He wondered if the console versions were better.

"How glitchy is the console version of Elder Scrolls online?"

"Glitchy, though not as bad as the PC version from what I hear. Sometimes characters vital to a mission disappear, making completion impossible. Missions that are free in Skyrim are DLC's, like the Thieves Guild. Trust me, it's a pain trying to do those missions when the guards don't die. So if you get caught, you're screwed. They're relentless. I canceled my subscription because of that. Too much headache. I don't like having to pay coin to travel outside of a way-shrine either, and don't get me started on the horses!"

He couldn't stop himself from laughing, and pain shot through his ribs. He pressed a hand to his side. Was it wrong to find her so cute when animated? He never met a woman so interested in gaming. Her brows drew in confusion.

"What's so funny?"

"Nothing, I'd just like to try gaming with you."

She chuckled.

"Nah. I get too into it and swear like a trooper. Nearly broke one of my games because if that. Well, my mother found it entertaining at least. Used to visit me to watch me play because it made her laugh."

Quiet Cassidy getting angry over a video game. That had to be a sight to see. A smile spread across his face, but quickly faded as he watched her pale looking in the rear-view mirror. Before he had a chance to ask what's wrong, she slammed the brakes and spun around the next corner.

"Hold on." She muttered.

He peered back to see a black Elantra turning and speeding after them. She gripped the wheel tightly, knuckles transparent white, and turned another corner. Blood rushed through his veins in a frenzy of fear and confusion.

"What's going on?" She grimaced.

"I suppose I should explain, but after we get out of this."

The vehicle once again caught up to her. She spun into a restaurant parking lot, then circled around back to a rear exit and rushed out, narrowly escaping collision with a truck. Whipping around the first corner leading to a subdivision, she zigzagged through the streets until their pursuer was out of sight. After finding a driveway that led behind a house, she drove in and parked in the back.

Sweat beaded her face as relief washed over her. Who was that? Why was he following her? He watched the color return to her complexion as she loosened her grip on the wheel and leaned back. While she struggled to catch her breath he pressed on with questions. He had no patience to wait for answers.

"What the hell just happened? Who was that?"

She tilted toward him, head never lifting off the headrest.

"My ex. I think he's a little crazy."

No kidding...

"Don't worry, he doesn't know where you live. I'd never let it happen."

"Don't you think you should have told me this? What if he interferes with...?"

"He won't! I won't let him." He shook his head.

"If he's stalking you, that's a big problem. He knows the car you drive. Why not get another vehicle?"

Perhaps that was callous. He didn't care. Somehow he had to survive long enough to regain his memory.

"Unaffordable." How could she not? Didn't she own the house she lived in?

"You can borrow mine!" Instant regret took hold. Nobody touched his Lexus, his pride and joy.

If his family and friends heard him, they'd lose their minds, or say he lost his.

"I'm not borrowing your car." That should have been a relief, but wasn't.

"Why not? At least then your problems won't carry into mine!" Her eyes narrowed, darkened.

"Because *your* enemy might recognize *your* car. Then what? I'm no stunt driver! All I have is basic driver training for the public."

A valid point.

"Why not rent one?" She shook her head.

"Again, unaffordable."

An interfering ex posed a big problem. She bit her lip, deep in thought.

"I suppose I can borrow my mothers'. She has a car and truck. I'll just hide this in her garage. That might work."

"Good, do that. We can't afford any interference." A nod was her only response.

They made their way to South Portland, ensuring they weren't followed, to a cute white bungalow with attached garage in a small subdivision. She flipped her visor to reveal a small device and pushed the button.

The garage door creaked open, revealing only one vehicle. A black Chevy Charger. *Nice.* She pulled in alongside it and jumped out.

"Come on, let's go." Pocketing her keys she swapped vehicles, retrieving a set of keys from the glove compartment.

Something seemed off. Without permission this was theft. Why didn't Cassidy call her mother? He followed, easing into the passenger seat and tossing his gym bag in the back. It still maintained that new car smell. The woman must have meticulously cared for the car. He propped his can across the back seat.

"Aren't you going to call and ask first?" Her eyes widened, but she schooled her features.

"It's fine, really. Nothing to worry about."

He stiffened. Last thing he needed was a charge for being an accomplice to grand theft auto. She must have sensed his hesitation.

"I'm allowed, stop worrying."

As she pulled out of the garage, she pressed a button on the ceiling, near the rear-view mirror. The radio played a Green Day song. When September Ends. A good song from a time before they sold out. She lowered the volume.

"What's wrong with that song?" She ignored him, nearly making it out of the driveway when a short, middle-aged brunette with graying hair approached, and knocked on the window.

A frown formed on her face. She rolled it down.

"Hi Sandra. Sorry I can't talk right now. I'm in a bit of a hurry."

She waited as Sandra spoke. He picked up a few words. Something about her mother, tea, and some kind of accident. Cassidy panicked. No doubt, she was hiding something.

"We can talk about this later. I have to go."

The women bent to see inside.

"I'm sorry. I didn't realize you were going on a date! Here I am ruining your evening by talking about the negative."

"It's OK." She forced a smile.

"Where are you two going?" Cassidy appeared lost.

"What's the name of that place we're going to again, babe?"

Babe, that rolled off her tongue too easy, but from her it sounded right.

"Back Bay Grill."

"Good choice. That's one of my favorite restaurants. You're so brave to be dealing with such hardship, Cassy. You deserve to unwind. Here." Sandra pulled a fifty from her jeans pocket, offering it to Cassidy who promptly refused.

"Thank you, but I can't accept that." The woman placed the money in Cassidy's hand, then closed her fingers over it.

"We go back a long time, and I've worked with your mother over thirty years. She'd want you to take care of yourself at least once in a while." Cassidy became sheet white. What was she dealing with that was so hard? What happened to her mother?

"Thank you." She murmured, sullen.

"Don't mention it. Nobody has done more for your mother than you. Have a good time, dear." Sandra leaned in once more.

"You treat her good, she's an angel." He wanted to get to the bottom of this.

"I will. What happened to her mother?"

Cassidy piped in immediately.

"Sorry, we *really* should get there before the rush."

She waved at Sandra.

"Thanks again!" She rolled the window up and backed onto the street.

He crossed his arms. What the hell was that? What did she not want him to know? Not being trusted was a hard pill to swallow.

"Is there something you want to tell me?" She refused to acknowledge his stare.

"Nope, nothing to talk about." She turned up the radio.

Evanescence screamed 'All That I'm Living For' through the speakers. Her fingers tapped the steering wheel to the beat. What hardened her so much that she'd close herself off from him? They used to be such good friends. Was this somehow his fault?

Only the music from the radio broke the silence as she drove. There was no wrapping his head around her. At lunch, her reaction to him, she might have let on it was an act, but he didn't sense that. All the more reason why her freezing him out made no sense. Either he read her wrong, or something else was going on. Her conflicting behavior had him stumped.

Chapter Nine

Cassidy

There was no getting back fast enough. She didn't want pity, especially Chase's. All she wanted to do was get in, hide in a corner, and let the earth ingest her whole. Chase followed some distance behind.

"Cassidy, wait." she kept going, nearly at the door.

"Cassidy, stop!" She didn't notice the trip wire until it snagged the hem of her pant leg. Before she knew it, a force slammed her body to the ground. Explosions sounded distant in her ringing ears as the house erupted in flames.

Her mind drifted in a haze. She couldn't get up. It took a moment for her senses to return and realize Chase had her pinned. Whatever happened to him, he never lost his reflexes.

She groaned as fiery pain roared in her head. Putting her hand to the back of her head, she discovered a lump, and something warm. Checking her hand she saw blood. Chase rose quickly.

"You OK?" He extended a hand to her, which she ignored.

She wasn't some weak damsel, she was Cassidy. Strong enough to endure a lifetime of hell and survive the worst pain imaginable. Able to take care of herself, her mother, everyone, everything, on her own, as always.

"I'm fine." Her vision blurred as she attempted to stand and her knees buckled.

He caught her as she collapsed, focusing weight on his good leg, pulling her up the length of him. His arms were vice-like as he pinned her against him. His warmth seeped into her. A hiss escaped him and his chest tightened.

Even while his pain was obvious, he hesitated to release her. His eyes darkened, and the storm raging behind them frightened her. Volatility emanated from him, threatening to ignite her from within. His mouth was dangerously close to hers, his breath like fire.

With a low growl he backed away slowly, eyes like molten marble. Her body protested. She stood, still woozy. He turned, watched the inferno. She wanted to cry.

This was her fault. If only she had listened. She should have refused the job. Then Chase would still have a home. Tears and guilt flooded her. It didn't matter that most of her possessions were in there with his. It was the least she deserved.

Chase pulled out his cell and called 911 while she contacted Mercer. He'd fire her. No way he wouldn't. What about her mother? Her stupidity cost so much!

"Hello, Miss Macayla."

With unsteady voice she told him what happened.

"It's not your fault. You're not trained to look for these things. Agent Averey has insurance, it'll be fine. The most important thing is you two are safe. Where's Agent Averey now?"

"He's on the phone with emergency services." She glance over to see his back facing her. His Sergeant may have forgiven her, but would he?

"Put him on the line."

She approached cautiously, fearing his reaction as she tapped his shoulder. His hardened expression filled her with fear. She raised the phone before her as though that could spurn his wrath. With a curious look he took the phone.

"Yes, Sir?"

Cassidy wrapped her arms around herself, rubbing them against a nervous chill. Would Chase keep her if told to? Would he forgive her? She wanted to run, hide. It would be a miracle if Chase spoke to her again after this.

"It appears whoever did this used clear fishing line as a trip wire, gained entry, possibly through a front window, and set explosives around the house." She watched as he listened to the voice penetrating his ear.

"Agreed. Must have been watching for some time, knew we left and how much time they had to set up." Another pause.

"There are depressions in the grass leading to a front window and the door."

She held her breath, heart drumming wildly. Peering up at the near cloudless sky, she wished it would rain. Her focus returned to him.

How did he remain so calm while her insides were chaotic, drowning in a sea of guilt, anxiety, and fear? How could someone do something so cold, so evil? Reprehensible! Yet there he stood, so focused it scared her.

"Yes, Sir. We'll go there." His features became grim.

"I don't blame her. She wouldn't have known, or seen the wire." A lump formed in her throat.

"Understood. Thank you, Sir." he disconnected the call and handed her the phone.

"We're going to a secure location. You can't know how to get there so you'll be blindfolded."

That didn't sit well with her at all. Nor did it make sense, nothing did. What had Jim gotten her into?

"I thought you weren't allowed to drive because of your meds! What if you have a seizure? Why trust me with the location of your superior, but not this?"

Impatience seeped into his features.

"It's top secret and is the Sergeant Major's personal emergency safe-house. It has a weapons cache and food reserves, underground greenhouse with a self-regulated system, and power derived from solar."

No! No! No!

"You don't need me if that's the case."

He ran a hand over his head in frustration.

"Look, whoever did this more than likely thinks we're dead. We don't want them knowing otherwise. The fact they knew we left, and for how long, tells me they've been watching and are aware of you."

This wasn't happening.

"You can leave me in town. I don't care. I have many important things to deal with and can't if I'm trapped in the middle of nowhere."

He crooked an eyebrow.

"Like your mother?" Damn it! Why'd he have to be so observant?

"Whoever did this learned about your life and hardships. The best chance for both of you is for you to play dead. Besides, if they know you're alive, they'll know I am. That puts us, our families, our friends in jeopardy. If we need anything, it will be taken care of by him."

She started shaking. It wasn't fair. This whole thing was insane, and while younger Cassidy would have been ecstatic, adult Cassidy was beyond apprehensive. She protested again, but he raised a hand and interjected.

"This is a matter of national security, so it trumps anything you think is important. That includes whatever is going on with your mother."

The world spun. She fell to her knees. He offered a hand once more. This was too much.

"I... I need a minute."

She dialed the doctor's number with shaky fingers. If nothing else, she had to make sure her mother was safe.

"Who are you calling?"

"A doctor."

He handed her the phone from his pocket. She eyed him with uncertainty.

"It's a private line. Don't use it for anything else and don't stay on more than a minute."

She accepted meekly.

"Thank you."

The situation left her asphyxiated by inexperience and fear. Somehow she forced herself to breathe. Next time she saw Jim, he'd pay for this.

"Doctor Hartman's office." A familiar voice.

"It's Cassidy Macayla calling."

"Miss Macayla. Checking on your mother today?" She gulped at her anxiety.

"How is she doing?"

"Her condition is unchanged. I'm actually glad you called. An opening has come up and we'll operate on her next Monday."

The best news she'd received in a while.

"That's great, thank you. I need to ask something of you."

"What is it?"

"Would you mind checking in on her more often than once per hour? Maybe even move her to a room in front of a nurses' station?"

Dead air hung between them for a few seconds. He knew she wasn't one for making strange requests.

"Something wrong?" She hesitated.

"Not much I can say. The nature of my job may have put her in danger and I want to make sure nothing happens to her."

He sighed.

"This would be an added expense, and I'd hate for you to pay more than necessary, but I'm also aware you've worked hard to ensure her care. If that's what you want, I'll see what I can do." She groaned inwardly. She'd be paying this for the rest of her life.

"Please do, doctor. I wouldn't ask without good reason. I won't be able to visit for some time, and this is the best I can do."

His deep voice softened in concern.

"I'll do what I can. Take care, Miss Macayla." She handed the phone back to Chase.

"Another thing. I need to commandeer your mothers' vehicle. Since she's apparently in the hospital, I bet she won't need it."

She wanted to punch him. The least he could have done was ask. Yet despite her anger, she couldn't help feel some pity, and awe. Before her stood the soldier, a man obstinate, focused, calculating, and cunning. In his eyes shone a hardened edge, a predator, and she didn't envy the enemy. Here she was falling apart.

She let his strength and resolve seep into her. Never did she want to appear weak before him, desiring only to be a woman worthy of his respect. In her teen years, he was one of the few who carried her through the darkest times, even though he had no clue what she endured. Unfortunately, by the time she sank to the deepest levels of darkness, they'd stopped talking.

She shook away the dismal thoughts. Here and now, there was a mission, a plan, and she didn't want to screw up more than she had already. Hopefully, his driving didn't get them killed.

"What now?"

He removed his shirt. She averted her gaze. It still amazed her there wasn't a long line of women knocking on his door. She bet if he so desired, he could etch more notched in his bed posts than Charlie Sheen had female co-stars.

"When we get in the car, I'll cover your eyes with this. You won't be able to see anything until we get there."

She started toward the car.

"How can you be sure where it is if it's so top secret?" Surely he wouldn't relay that information over the phone.

"He told me."

He must have picked up on her scrutiny.

"Don't worry, no one else knows. We use a complex linguistic code."

She sat in the front passenger seat.

"What about your physio? Your meds?" Sirens echoed in the distance. His movements quickened.

"I can manage on my own. If I need medication, Mercer will take care of it. If there are any more questions, they'll have to wait. We have to go."

His hands were firm but gentle as he wrapped the blue shirt around her head, covering her eyes. He folded it over several times, making it impossible to see through. Perhaps it was the adventurous side of her talking, but under different circumstances, this might be interesting.

Her hands pressed against the fabric, adjusting for comfort. His hands covered hers, making sure it was secure enough. The jolt from contact left her insides buzzing.

"Is it comfortable?" She lowered her hands to her lap.

"It's fine."

Her other senses heightened, and the gentle aroma of soap emanating from the fabric seemed enhanced. A spicy, masculine smell. After closing the door he ran around to the other side. She fished the keys from her pocket and held them out. After closing the door on his side, he took them.

Her skin prickled warmly as he leaned over and buckled her in. His spicy scent and steady teased her senses, sending a sizzling surge to her abdomen. She sucked in a breath and stiffened, biting her lip to fight the temptation to lean forward, so hard she tasted blood.

"Are you alright?"

"Yeah, I'm OK."

"You sure? You look a little flushed." His tone reflected amusement, but she'd never admit anything, even if her life depended on it.

"I'm fine." Her voice didn't sound as strong as she'd hoped. She swore she heard him chuckle quietly.

Sirens got closer as he drove away. It nearly deafened her when they passed but served as a welcome distraction. Long ago, she'd have followed anywhere he wanted. Perhaps she did the same now, only for completely different reasons.

The drive continued on forever. His loud, melodic ringtone made her jump, and the car slowed to a stop. She appreciated a conscientious driver. He grumbled.

Rather than answer he took off again. Awkwardness filled the air, yet she feared breaking the silence. Her stomach however, didn't. Chase mumbled inaudibly.

"Sorry." She squirmed, sheepish. He exhaled softly.

"Another hour to go, I need a break, anyway. What would you like to eat?"

She just wanted to quiet her stomach, she didn't care how.

"Is there anywhere you want to go?"

"Don't matter as long as it's quick, a drive-thru preferably. You'll need to take that off your head for a minute or it'll draw too much attention."

Remembering his bare upper body she nipped her lower lip. That would also draw attention from women in the area, likely followed by wary boyfriends and husbands.

"I imagine you'll want to wear this anyway." Hopefully he didn't realize she'd been eyeing him since yesterday like an oasis in the desert.

The comment seemed to irritate him more than anything.

"Yes, right." She flinched at his harsh tone.

"I didn't mean..."

"Don't worry about it." He snapped.

She frowned. *Foot in mouth, Cassidy. Foot. In. Mouth.* She bit her tongue. A long stretch of silence followed.

"Well? What do you want?"

"Not sure. Chicken salad might be nice." She felt around for her purse until she found it.

"Don't bother, I'll pay." She didn't like that idea and opened her mouth to protest, but he cut her off.

"I want to." So badly she wanted to return the favor someday, but dreadful foreboding warned otherwise.

"Thank you."

"Don't mention it." Nothing was said for the remainder of the drive. When he liberated her from the makeshift blindfold, it took a while for her eyes to adjust.

There were no visible signs to indicate their location. Chase undoubtedly chose this place on purpose. He went through the Subway drive-thru, ordered himself a meatball sub, and her a grilled chicken salad, along with two bottles of water. They then parked and ate.

The same ringtone as before sang from his pocket. Checking the caller ID he grumbled before answering.

"Hello." The curtness of his greeting surprised her.

She tried to continue eating but his displeasure felt tangible. At the point he spoke something about getting back together or not that her discomfort intensified. His business was just that, *his* business. Whatever her feelings, she only wanted him happy.

Desiring to give him privacy she placed the salad on the dash and opened the door to step out. Halfway out, Chase grabbed her arm. Confused, she turned her head. A shake of a disapproval greeted her. Was he scared she'd run off? Or did he think she'd draw too much attention? He leaned over and shut the door.

"That was a car door." Cassidy wriggled, tense.

"I was driving. What does it matter? You call now, after what you did?" What she wouldn't give to be anywhere else.

"Well thanks for your concern. I'm really busy now. Bye." He hit end and whipped the phone in the glove compartment, closing with a slam.

Words failed her. Grabbing the remains of her food she focused on finishing that. His eyes burned into her. She tried to ignore their intensity. *I'm not going to ask. I'm not going to ask...*

"She cheated on me, then took off with the other guy around the time I found out about my next deployment."

Cassidy nearly choked. Who'd ever cheat on him? If it were her, she'd do anything to make him happy. It was common knowledge those relationships were difficult to maintain, but she couldn't imagine. Perhaps she was biased, he wasn't exactly an angel, but even with his stubborn streak, it seemed foolish.

"Not sure what to say. I'm sorry."

He sighed as his eyes adjusted downward.

"I suppose I must have driven her to it or something. Not giving her enough attention. Something like that. It wouldn't really be right to blame her when I had my part in it too."

Cassidy tried to force the lump from her throat, to no avail. She understood wanting someone's attention after not seeing them for a long time, she'd missed Chase like crazy, but that didn't excuse the woman's behavior. It didn't have to resort to that.

Didn't help that witnessing her parent's rocky marriage skewed her point of view. Her mother endured infidelity, and also gross manipulation and countless beatings until her father died. He hadn't cheated because of anything her mother did either, but possessed a flawed sense of entitlement. The so-called man didn't treat his children any better.

Chase's problems sounded more like a proper flow of communication may have prevented a lot of bad decisions and heartache. What did she know, other than he shouldn't shoulder all the blame?

Since childhood she learned much about what love is and isn't. What her parents had wasn't. What she discovered was love is an action, not just an emotion. It's how she understood what she felt about Chase. She'd have taken a beating or a bullet for him in a heartbeat.

At the same time she held nothing in the way of beauty, and doubt affected every decision she made. Her only hope was to find someone to appreciate her as is and overlook her sordid past, one filled with more bad decisions than stars in the sky.

"I get her sense of neglect since you go away for long stretches of time, but surely things could have gone differently. I'm sorry, but your work is important, and you need time to yourself too. This is a tough one."

One thing about her, she wasn't a home-wrecker. He mumbled before changing the subject.

"We should get going. The Sergeant will meet us there and we don't want to get there late."

Inside, she face palmed. Another foot-in-mouth moment. Why did he even talk to her? Even as a friend he was out of her league.

She plugged the MP3 player from her purse into the jack in the center console before Chase had the shirt over her head once more. As Schism played, she lamented her words.

The rest of the drive went on without a word. No doubt he regretted having her there. He should have left her behind to manage her own problems. She screwed up bad this time, and there wasn't a cave in the world deep enough for her to hide in.

Chapter Ten

Chase

Why did she have to be so supportive, understanding? Acknowledging both sides but still defending him. He remembered when he first got together with Rachel. Everyone told him she was too young. Cassidy only cared that she did good to him and made him happy.

There was something amid the words she spoke that night. Something between the lines. He'd only seen her for five minutes the whole night before she disappeared like a thief in the night. He wished he'd had more time with her before she left.

Confusion festered. His emotions terrified him. He sensed something between them, which became more apparent after the explosion. He could have dismissed what happened at lunch, especially due to her comment about his bare chest, yet when he buckled her in... That wasn't his imagination, was it? Were the mixed signals all in his head? Why did she avoid looking at him every time the shirt came off?

His jaw tensed. He tried for an outward display of confidence but inside it was lacking. For whatever reason, Cassidy got to him. In the last twenty-four hours her presence sent his world into a tailspin. It was getting far too difficult to keep his hands off her.

Yeah, what happened pissed him off. In fact, it made his blood boil. Whoever did this would pay dearly. In the end, those things were replaceable, and they'd expected it to happen anyway, just not so soon.

Then there was Cassidy. He didn't want to lose her. While he had his mission, get out of sight, regain his memory, stay alive, he wanted to keep her safe. How could he when he wasn't a hundred percent?

Then there was his memory. It wasn't simply a matter of things he personally saw and heard, but locations, files, pictures, people, places, enough information to cause a blow in a massive enemy network. Only he knew the location of these things, locked away in a brain incapable of remembering shit.

The rest of the trip was quiet, but his mind wouldn't stop. Why didn't she trust him? What did she fear from him? Using his non-driving leg was difficult, but not as much as trying to figure out what Cassidy was holding in the rest of the ride. He couldn't interpret the anxiety pouring from her the rest of the ride.

They made it to the gate with about a half-hour to spare. The massive construct appeared as secure as Fort Knox. He punched the code into the console beside the massive black iron gates and they opened.

As much of a stronghold as it appeared, nothing was impenetrable. If the enemy wanted in bad enough, they'd find a way. He was banking on the world thinking him dead long enough for a miracle to happen. If only a battle would bring it out, hopefully Cassidy would work one for him. He thought that, though he really didn't believe in miracles.

He heaved a sigh of relief after parking in the garage.

"We're here." He shut off the car.

His fingers tingled as they grazed her soft skin while removing the shirt from over her eyes. Pity filled him. This wasn't what he wanted for her, but an order was an order.

At least he had permission to access everything, including weapons. He drooled a little at the idea of checking out the artillery cache, one thing he liked about his job, after realizing his enthusiasm for firearms. That, and the adrenaline rush of combat.

"I still don't understand why you brought me here. I'm pretty useless at this point." She crossed her arms.

He wanted to assuage her uneasiness and fear, but the solution eluded him.

"Let's have a look around. My legs need a stretch."

She nodded and followed. The evening air had chilled, and he wished he had a sweater, something to keep warm. Cassidy rubbed her arms with a shiver.

"You want in the car?" She shook her head.

"I'm fine. I'm sure the walk will help."

"Would you like my shirt?" He'd grown accustomed to temperature changes, and it wouldn't be for long anyway.

"No, really, I'm OK. Thanks."

It shouldn't have surprised him. She had a stubborn streak nearly as long as his. As they walked, the chill didn't dissipate from her. In moments her already light skin paled more. He wrapped an arm around her, using his hand to rub some warmth into her cool flesh, but she only shivered more.

"Thanks Chase, but that's not necessary." In spite of what she said, she didn't shrug him away. Was that good or was she colder than she let on?

He relaxed, wondering if she also felt the surge of electricity running between them. Time stood still as they walked the path lined with flowers and shrubs which led to the back door. The setting sun painted the sky a pastel feast for the eyes. A beautiful work of art. They sat on the steps.

"What will you do for physio now?" Her voice came out timid.

"I don't know."

"You allowed to spar?" The question threw him off. He wasn't sure if that would help, but hell, why not try?

"Could give it a shot."

She folded her hands over her lap.

"OK. I'll spar with you, but I don't know everything you do. So I probably won't provide much of a challenge." He smiled.

"That's fine. I won't teach you anything either."

She smiled. Bright, beautiful, tempting.

"That's fine." Looking in those emerald orbs made the world seem far away. The air was electric.

A slight breeze brushed honey-blond strands across her should and he couldn't resist sweeping them back. She shivered and scanned his face, stopping at his lips. A silent plea impossible to ignore.

A hand found its way up, cupping the base of her jaw, easing her toward him. Her breath quickened in anticipation before his mouth captured hers. As he did, her breath hitched, and with a sigh she relaxed into him.

If he ever wondered what she felt about him, the answered lay in her response as she relinquished control to his gentle onslaught. He ran a hand through silken strands and tugged, deepening the kiss. His appetite became voracious, but he subdued himself. His reward was a pleading moan that had his blood, his body, roaring to life.

She clutched lightly at his shirt. The way she did it told him a wild cat lay within, waiting to escape. The idea left his body pulsing. His insides groaned in protest when a gruff cough broke the spell.

A flustered Cassidy greeted him, lips swollen, eyes darkened with desire. Who'd have thought she held so much passion behind such a passive, distant facade? Her mouth didn't lie, and he bet her hips wouldn't either, assuming he ever got the chance to find out. He bet he could spend a lifetime at it with her and never bore, but it would all mean nothing if she didn't trust him.

"Nice to see you two getting along."

He rushed to his feet, ignoring the ache in his leg, unable to ignore the other. He wasn't used to seeing the man in casual attire. Raising a hand to his head he offered a salute.

"Hello, Sir."

"Take your seat, son. I only need to see one at attention."

A soft chuckle from behind him tickled his ears while he did as instructed. How embarrassing.

"I'll show you around, then give you the key. Honestly, I don't expect the enemy to just give up when they realize there were no bodies at the scene."

"I don't understand. Why send us here? Why am I here?" Cassidy's voice came out laced with frustration.

"Jim tells me you're resourceful, quick to act, even in stressful situations. If Chase needs help, he'll need someone who won't freeze up under pressure. Right now, that's more valuable to me than someone who can fire an HK416."

"But this place is like a fortress! Who could ever hope to get in here?"

To the untrained eye the Sergeant Major seemed calm, but he could tell the man was working for patience. He wasn't used to someone questioning him.

"We're dealing with an enemy within a large network of varied resources and intelligence. Once they discover this location, and that Chase is here, it's only a matter of time before they gain entry. You need to understand that anything can, and probably will happen, and he might not regain his memory before then."

"This is your place. Why offer it up so freely?"

"In the interest of national security. The information locked away in Chase's mind is of vital importance. It's all I can say."

Mercer's impatience grew, and he wanted to get started with the tour. He retrieved his cane and cut in before she could ask another question. If she found out what awaited, she'd turn tail and run. Most would. These weren't just schoolyard bullies but militant men who desired to deliver death and leave destruction in their wake.

"Let's get going then."

Mercer gave an affirmative nod.

"Right."

Inside, everything seemed sterile and bare. Even the kitchen. Mostly basic furniture in each room save for the living area, which contained a rather large television, blue-ray player, and computer. All the tables were thick, metallic, yet still stylish.

"The internet runs on a private, secure server." Chase nodded. They followed to another room, halfway up a hall, to a nature painting centered on the back wall.

"This is something I'm sure you'll appreciate, Chase."

He stood ready, anticipating the reveal. Mercer slipped a finger along the frame, stopped at one corner until he heard a click, and moved on to another. Once all four corners were activated, a grinding sound from his left grabbed his attention. There was no mistaking Cassidy's sharp intake of breath.

"Each corner has a switch. After two minutes the case will close and the switches will return to the off position."

They approached the alcove housing several weapons. He scanned them all, from grenades and handguns to rifles and machine guns, hovering on the M202 FLASH, his favorite. That thing could make a statement. Just the thought of holding it had his adrenaline surging.

Knives, swords, and ammo lined the bottom portion of the alcove. A treasure trove unlike any other. He wanted to test everything.

Cassidy's delicate fingers traced over the handguns as if getting to know them intimately. She didn't seem interested in anything larger. He tried not to think about how much he wished he was the R1 Remington her fingertip lingered on right then. She seemed especially impressed by the attached silencer.

"Is there a cool down period to open it again?"

"Thirty seconds."

"OK."

"Now over here..." They followed to the opposite wall. "You'll see how to activate the entrance downstairs."

Cassidy's confusion was apparent until Mercer lifted the third floor panel from the wall and pushed the concealed button. A popping sound came from somewhere nearby.

"Follow me." On the floor in the closet beside them was a trap door, now open.

"Wow! This is just like a Nancy Drew novel!" He never realized she liked to read. She withdrew sheepishly from his curious stare.

"My grandfather used to buy them for me as a child. They were my favorite books."

The more he learned, the more intrigued he became. She was more complex than he though.

"Right." The Sergeant interjected. "This is the entrance to the lower level where the self-sustained greenhouse is. There's a whole other living space down there. The whole thing serves as a bomb shelter." They proceeded down the steep metal stairs.

It was massive, like an underground mansion. Every room was bright, with white walls, and well furnished. One of them maintained an impressive security station, nearly an entire wall clustered full of monitors. Each one displayed a different part of the property, inside and out. Past the kitchen area, a door opened to reveal a gargantuan greenhouse. It's size rivaled that of the bomb shelter itself.

The irrigation system was impressive, and the variety of plants organized on tables and shelves was more than he could name.

"I had solar roofing tiles created for the roof, and there's other solar panels further out on the property. If you'll look to the ceiling, you'll see a long series of ultraviolet grow lights which span the entire length of the room. The sprinkler system is set on a timer so no need to worry about watering them." Walking to the back, Chase let out an impressed whistle.

"This place has everything necessary for self-sustainability. There are no genetically modified plants here. They're all pure stock, and no chemicals since there's no reason to use them."

They found themselves before a large black cabinet that took up half a wall.

"I keep the seeds in here." He watched the cabinet open, revealing a large assortment of seeds, gardening tools, and bags of soil and fertilizer.

"I've never dealt with greenhouse plants. Do you have to rotate them?" Cassidy's interest put a smile on Mercer's face. Clearly she'd hit a soft spot.

"It seems there are some omissions from your resume. No, they don't need rotated. Everything needed to measure and balance out the soil is in this cabinet."

"OK." Noticing his expression she smiled.

"I used to help my father with his garden."

He itched to inquire about it but this wasn't the time.

"Let's head back up." They obeyed.

After they returned to the cache room they were shown a solid, four inch thick metal barrier hidden behind the door.

"This might not keep them out for long, but it should buy you time to gather your weapons and get downstairs." It locked securely in the mechanism on the opposing wall.

Cassidy huffed.

"I still don't understand. You're hoping he'll regain his memory but that's not a guarantee, is it? Why put us here if we don't even know his memory is retrievable, or why your enemy would bother to come assuming he knows Chase has amnesia."

He caught that look, the one that said his patience had reached its limit. Chase opted to spare the man from explaining.

"Because I have Retrograde amnesia. As severe as my injuries were, the TBI is somewhere between mild and moderate, so it's not a matter of if, but when. Unfortunately, we don't know how to trigger the memory. Nothing we've done has worked." He ran a hand over his head. The concern on her face unsettled his nerves. How much should he tell? Last thing he wanted was to scare her.

"Every time I have a seizure I remember bits and pieces, but nothing big enough to get the vital info. It's come down to the possibility it might take something... bigger than usual."

Confusion gave way to fear and her eyes widened as an idea dawned on her. Perhaps she figured it out.

"No..." It came out a whisper.

He remained silent, allowing her a moment to register her thoughts. She stared through him, a variety of emotions playing across her face. Rather than yell, warn him of the potential consequences of such recklessness, she withdrew in defeat.

Without a word she pulled the barrier open and stormed out. Was she leaving?

"Cassidy, where are you going?"

"Give her some time."

Another door slammed, the front entrance.

"You two knew each other previously?"

Chase couldn't calm the anxiety overtaking him.

"We were friends in school. Haven't seen her since, til now."

A pause.

"Make sure she keeps focused. If she can, then she's better for this than I thought." That confused him. What did that mean? What did Mercer see that he didn't? "Motivation is key."

His confusion only grew. There was a warning in the man's eyes keeping him from asking.

"You stay here. I have to get some things from my car."

Suddenly he found himself alone with his thoughts. What the hell was going on?

Chapter Eleven

Cassidy

She sat in the Charger, fuming. She should have known. There were no accidents, no coincidences when it came to the army and what they did. Everything needed planned, calculated, controlled. What happened to Chase's home wasn't a matter of if, but when. Mercer, Chase, they both knew.

She plugged her music player to the jack in the console and Face the Pain bled threw the speakers. She banged the side of the steering wheel with a clenched fist. This whole time they hoped something would happen, but only on their terms.

Knowing the evil inclinations of their enemy they put her, her mother, and her friends at risk. If she returned home, would she get overlooked or further risk her life and that of those she cared about, just as Chase suggested?

This wouldn't be like a home invasion with only a couple of people either, she was sure. Why else would it necessitate her being in a place with such a thick metal barrier and enough weapons and ammunition to take down half an army? They expected a party, a big one, and she happened to be an unfortunate invitee. This would somehow jog Chase's memory? Insane!

Why not use a simulation? Would that not have the same effect, or did they try that already? An endless loop of questions rolled around in her head, which only increased her ire.

Memories of her childhood surfaced. The home where she grew up, the neglect, violence, and psychological trauma she endured. She'd shed tears far too often, some nights even blood. Meeting Chase had helped. Without knowledge of her ordeal he'd brought out the best in her, inspired her bravery in spite of the hopelessness of the situation, just being the unique person he was.

She pressed her fingers to her lips. The kiss. All her life she thought he didn't want her. Could she have been wrong the entire time? Did he truly care? Or did he only seek carnal pleasure?

If he did care, he'd only disappear after discovering the things she'd done in his absence. He wasn't perfect, but he was still far more than she deserved. She was only one small fish in the ocean, he could do better.

With a sigh she ran her fingers through her hair, agonizing over what to do. Even while the betrayal that they'd concealed this plan from her lingered, she couldn't abandon her position. Her mother, Chase, they both needed her.

Knowing the potential outcome she needed to speak the Mercer, make sure her mother had all her needs met. Lost in thought, she didn't notice his approach. The knock on her window startled her. After turning down the music she rolled it down.

"I expected you two needed supplies, so I made a stop on the way." He handed her a large, weighty gym bag, which she examined hurriedly. Toiletries, hair ties, clothing.

"Thank you." His stern expression dissuaded her grateful smile.

"And Miss Macayla..." His tone didn't fill her with confidence.

"Yes?"

"In battle, emotions can seem overwhelming. Let it feed your determination, don't let it overwhelm you."

"Yes, Sir." Did this have to do with what he saw at the stairs?

"Sergeant, I assume you are expecting something big. Could I ask a favor?"

"Go on..."

She sighed, envisioning her mother.

"If something happens to me, I want my pay to cover as much of my mothers' care as possible."

"Ah, yes. I know about that." Her eyes widened. "I did a small background check on you. Had I been more thorough, I'd have known you and Chase had a history. It's of little relevance, and I trust Jim."

History? She wanted to laugh.

"We were only friends in school." He leaned in.

"Just keep focused. We need that information and can't afford mistakes."

She swallowed against the lump forming in her throat. Why did everyone suddenly feel the need to remind her to do her job?

"Understood, Sir."

"Good." He backed away. "There's more inside for you guys. Can't have your skills going to mush." Her brows scrunched in confusion.

"Also, I still expect those updates." A slight tilt of her head indicated her understanding.

"I'll speak with you later."

She ran her fingers through her hair. Surely she wouldn't have just gotten that lecture if her feelings weren't so transparent. At least to Mercer. Could Chase sense them too? He'd never toy with her affections, would he?

Something just outside the edges of her mind loomed. She couldn't put her finger on it, but knew it involved Chase. Another big reason for the distancing between them. She shook it away, sure it was better off forgotten. The ringing of her phone cut into her thoughts.

Stacy's name and number flashed across the screen.

"Hey! What's up?"

"You never came home last night. We were worried. Marc only told me a little. What's going on?"

She ran a hand through her hair once more.

"I can't say much but I'm on assignment. Not the usual kind either. This is big."

"How big? Are you in some kind of trouble? You can tell me!"

She gulped. Oh, she was in trouble alright. Way over her head in a surreal set of circumstances that by all logic, shouldn't happen. If she wasn't living it, she'd never have believed it possible.

"I'm sorry, I can't say more than that. Don't worry about me, I'm fine." She hoped she sounded more convincing than she felt. Nothing about any of this was fine.

"We've been friends for years, Cassy. I can tell when you're scared. You're not fooling me." She sighed.

"I really can't say anything about this. It's a very big deal. One wrong move and people might get hurt."

"Oh God! Cassidy! What have you gotten yourself into?"

"Stacy, please stop worrying about me. I can't stay on the phone anymore but I'll call you and Marc as soon as I can."

"Cassidy!"

Chase's reflection appeared in her rear-view mirror, still some distance away.

"I'm sorry. I have to go. Bye."

Stacy yelled her name once more as she hung up. No doubt they were worried sick and angry with her. No help for that at the moment. She needed to remain focused. She'd just gotten out of her car when she received an incoming text.

Steve...

As she read the message, she clutched the handle of her bag so hard, her knuckles turned a translucent white. There was no stopping the angry tremors.

It seems you got over me rather quickly, didn't you? Who's the guy in the car with you? You really think I'm going to give up? Maybe a chat with your friends will clear things up. I'll be seeing you.

Ice coursed through her veins. Was he serious? So if the terrorists weren't already a threat to them, Steve was. She wanted to scream, punch things, kick things.

"Steve, is it?" She spun quickly. Chase was stealthy, she'd give him that. He left her wondering how he bridged the gap so quickly without a sound. "That's the ex who followed you?"

She frowned.

"Yeah. We only dated a few months and haven't seen each other in as long, if not longer. He cheated, then hit me when I called him on it. That's when I called it off."

His features turned grim.

"Looks like he just threatened something against your friends."

"I need to warn them." She started dialing.

"It might be an empty threat. More than likely, he's trying to bait you. You'll make them worry for nothing."

Her blood boiled. Clearly he'd never been on the receiving end of that kind of crazy.

"What if you're wrong? What if something happens to them?"

His jaw tensed.

"Warn them if you must, but be quick about it. Too long on the phone if it's being monitored and it'll give away everything."

She shook her head.

"What does it matter? You're expecting them to find us anyway." His grip on his cane tightened.

"It's all about timing."

Calling to warn them only made things worse. Now they were frantic for her. As always in life, everything was an uphill battle.

How kind of Mercer to bring in sparring supplies and a punching bag. She had a lot of negative energy to dispel. It might not solve any problems but at least it would help her keep in top form. She nearly cried for joy at the sight of everything, including the adjustable weights and laptop containing the best variety of no-nonsense martial art instructional videos. The athletic wear fit like a dream too. She had to hand it to the man, he'd really done his homework.

This was the kind of thing she'd missed in childhood. She'd wanted to take Tae Kwon Do but her father put the kibosh on that. Apparently swimming and gymnastics were perfectly fine, but anything allowing her to defend herself, unfathomable. Better late than never.

So focused on the kickboxing workout, the door opening startled her. She stopped and turned to see Chase watching intently. She wiped the sweat from her brows as he approached, a bit too interested in her activity.

"Remind me to stay on your good side." He chuckled.

Ever since the incident on the stairs she'd sensed a change in him. Or maybe her imagination had kicked in to overdrive. There was no imagining how he looked in his black shorts and matching shirt. To her amazement, he hadn't brought his cane.

"Were you ready to spar or did you want to wait til later?"

"I've never sparred with women before." She crooked a grin.

"There's a first time for everything."

"You're not worried?" She shook her head with a smile.

"In Muay Thai, nine times out of ten I was paired up with men."

"What if I punch you in the face or something?" Laughter escaped her.

"If you do you aren't the first, and likely not the last." If he only knew.

At least she could laugh about it now, which meant she was a far cry from where she used to be. Never again would she be a victim. If she had to fight, it would be on her terms. He gave her an odd look.

"Cassidy..." She placed her wrapped fists on her hips.

"Oh, come on! You're not too chicken to take on a woman like me, are you?"

He gave her an in depth scan, a wicked promise in his eyes.

"Is that a challenge?"

"Do you accept?"

"Sure." He retrieved a pair of boxing gloves from a gym bag in the corner, next to the well-worn beige couch. After putting them on, he clapped twice as he approached. She watched, curious.

"Aren't you going to stretch first? What about your leg?"

"Nah! This shouldn't take long."

Surely he was jesting. Not warming up and stretching before a workout could be harmful. He must consider her easy prey. He'd learn.

"Sure you don't want to warm up first? I won't go easy on you because you're injured." Maybe a little.

He bellowed. She rolled her eyes.

"Suit yourself." She adjusted her wraps before getting into combat stance. The look in his eyes told her he saw this as nothing more than child's play. He stretched his neck from side to side, bounced while still favoring his injured leg, and focused.

"Hooah! Ullamh!" It came out a deep roar.

Tribal, primitive. He clapped once more. How did anyone make such a noise? It had to be an intimidation tactic. Unfortunately for him, it didn't work. She placed her fists on her hips.

"What the hell was that?"

"What?" A disbelieving grin adorned her face as she shook her head.

"What you said. What's that supposed to mean?" He smirked.

"'Hooah' is basically a power word meant to energize people to become battle ready. 'Ullamh' is Gaelic for ready."

She didn't dare ask how many languages he spoke. She returned to her stance.

"OK. Let's get to it then."

"You're not scared?" His tone oozed humor. She giggled.

"It takes more than growling like a caveman to scare me." A strange expression crossed his face for a split-second but he said nothing. "On with it then?" He nodded.

Not surprising he countered every move, not that she was really trying. She wanted to gauge his reaction time first. That he had superior training in everything wasn't lost on her. At least she held the element of surprise, which she'd only be able to use once.

"Is that the best you can do?"

"Are you trying to bait me?"

"Is it working?"

"Bring it on!"

He went for a hook but she blocked, raised her knee to his abdomen while mindful of his bruise. She immediately followed by twisting his arm back and kicking her heel in the back of his good leg. She finished with an arm snug around his neck, legs wrapped around his back leg to absorb the shock as she fell backwards to the ground, locking her hold beneath his chin. Yeah, she couldn't do this again. The element of surprise had officially gone.

"Holy crap!" His voice sounded strained as she struggled to maintain the hold. He was a persistent force, without question, but she wasn't one to give up either.

"Sorry, but I think you're supposed to tap."

"Like hell I will." He tried to pry her arm away, but she clung tightly to the crook of her other arm. She then wrapped her legs around his waist, locking her ankles together to solidify her hold.

"I should probably warn you, chokes are my specialty." Her words came out a series of huffs. He muttered a long string of mostly inaudible swears.

"Just tap already. Come on. Who will know?"

Rather than reply he stood. She yelped in surprise and instinctively clung tighter to keep from falling. That didn't seem to phase him as he pried her ankles apart and flipped her. Before she could blink he was over her, pinning her wrists, a knee between her thighs, and a triumphant expression on his face. Something hard pressed against her hips and her insides stirred in response.

"You seem rather pleased with yourself." He tilted his head in agreement.

"You going to teach me that?"

"Nope."

"You're mean." A wicked grin formed on his face.

"I know."

She tried to get up, but he held her in place. His eyes darkened into molten pools that melted her insides.

"Chase?" She barely managed to whisper.

He leaned in, lips just brushing hers when he roared in pain. In less than a second he stood on his feet, clutching his recovering leg. It didn't take a genius to figure out why. He must have realized it too because he stared knowingly at her.

"You OK?"

"It's nothing, I'm fine."

"Anything I can...?"

"I said I'm fine!" His frustration rippled through her. She needed to get away before it consumed her.

"I need a shower." She removed her wraps, tossed them in the bag, and left.

Cool water kissed her flesh, rejuvenating her. As much as she enjoyed hot showers, cool ones were so much better post workout. Grabbing some shampoo, she lathered up her hair.

Confusion abound. This was the second time Chase made a move. Her cynical side refused to believe he'd ever want her. If he found out about her past, he'd turn tail and run.

After everything got washed, conditioned, and squeaky clean, she dried and dressed, then rushed to her room. After closing the door she jumped in the double bed, rolled on her back, and stared at the ceiling. To entertain the idea that Chase could ever love her was madness at best. Even if he did, she'd just screw it all up anyway. That seemed to be her *real* specialty.

With a sigh she whipped a pillow against the wall. She had to be crazy. Having been unable to get him out of her system, her memory, all this time, could only mean something was wrong with her. Being in his presence didn't help a bit.

Chapter Twelve

Chase

For the longest time he leaned against the wall facing her bedroom door, behind which she hid for at least an hour now. Unbelievable. She was not only much stronger than she appeared, also capable of more than just throwing a punch. No question he was stronger, better, faster. Yet she hid a stubborn ferocity, and her caring nature ran deeper than he imagined. He noticed her attentiveness, avoiding his ribs and cushioning his leg. To underestimate her would be far too easy.

The more he learned about her, the more he wanted her. She didn't nag or argue about his leg because he hadn't warmed up or stretched, and when he refused help, she let him be. Cassidy was an enigma.

Her voice echoed from beyond the door as she sang. Soft, melodic, more captivating than he remembered. His mind drifted to when Rita had dared her to get on her knees and sing to him. She'd been young, nervous, scared even. At the same time, she was gutsy. That had to be nothing short of humiliating. If she knew what rattled around in his head seeing her on her knees, she'd have run for the hills.

Then in the room earlier as they sparred, sweat glistening on that soft skin, it seared his blood and left him hard. She didn't realize her beauty, and he yearned to show a measure of what she ignited in him. Groaning inwardly, he made his way to the bathroom to release his pent-up tension.

As days passed, he grew dreadfully bored. Nothing to do, nowhere to go. He longed for the days when he'd run outside and play chicken with passing motorists. The boredom suffocated him and knowing something waited on the wind didn't solve the here and now.

The only thing that made the ordeal tolerable was Cassidy. Everything she cooked left him resisting the urge for seconds. His leg had improved, and he assumed working out with her helped.

The more time spent with her, the harder to keep from playing with fire. Catching her dancing to 'Rude Boy' in her room through the partially open door nearly killed him. Still she continued, unaware of his presence.

How long did it take for her to mimic every move? How limber was she? She'd clearly learned a few new moves over the years. When 'Everybody' by Rudenko came on and she arched her back, a hand grazing down the center of her body, followed by a body roll and tick of her right hip, he nearly ruined his shorts.

He knocked, coughing nervously. Her eyes widened in shock and she fell. Not even a hundred cold showers could undo what he saw. A lifetime of wanking material rolled into a few minutes. She stood quickly.

"What is it Chase?" Her eyes scanned him head to toe, hesitating at his chest and waist. She turned away swiftly, cheeks crimson, and nipped her lower lip.

His imagination conjured up at least a dozen different scenarios, all involving her in some very interesting positions. It caught his interest that she'd seen the evidence of his arousal but didn't berate him. Clearly she wanted him, but perhaps he needed to man up, because she wasn't one to initiate anything.

"Would you like to join me for a walk in the garden?" She stared curiously.

"Sure, just let me get washed up." She snatched some clothes and rushed past him.

He spied the video on the screen of her laptop. If she wanted, she could break hearts. If she were the type, he could be in every bit of trouble as the guy in the video, stuck in the hot seat.

They walked slowly. The cool evening air was electric. Light pastel colors painted the sky, an amazing backdrop against flourishing trees. Cassidy seemed into it, and the shimmering black tank top and matching long skirt really accentuated her figure.

She fidgeted.

"What's going on Chase?" He wasn't entirely sure, but put on an air of confidence.

He remembered long ago, the one and only time he'd flirted with her. In the club during teen dance night. They and their friends sat around the table when he got the bright idea to run his foot up and down her side, over her ribs. She'd been so stunned, she asked what he was doing. Even more so when he told her. From then until the next song he danced to, she sat perfectly still, except for the wringing of her fingers, like she had no idea what to do. She didn't tell him to stop, but didn't flirt in return. That remained one of the most confusing things he'd ever endured.

What would she do if he did something like that now? Would she remember? He was dying to find out.

He wrapped his arm around her waist, and let his thumb trail upward, strumming her ribs. The sharp hitch in her voice was unmistakable, something he'd never have noticed that night. He felt a fool for not noticing at the time.

"You didn't answer my question. What are you doing?"

"Flirting." Her mouth widened and she stopped, turned, gaped at him.

So she remembered. Those emerald orbs shone brightly.

"Chase?" She breathed.

Now is as good a time as any... He tried his best to appear confident while as nervous as a schoolboy.

"Cassidy, I was wondering... Would you like to, umm, get together?"

Her jaw hit the ground, her anxiety mounted.

"You... you want to go out with me?" Was that so hard to believe? He nodded. She was cute. Her facial expressions could put emoticons to shame. Her breath quickened, eyes peering around as if there might have been anyone else he meant to ask.

"Yeah. You're an amazing woman."

She narrowed her lids.

"No, I'm not." Not the expected reaction. His heart sank.

"So, no?" She snickered.

"Yes, I will, and no, I'm not amazing."

He forgot how she'd never been good with taking compliments.

"Honestly, you deserve better."

Her doing anything to make herself unworthy was unfathomable. It only raised more questions. He opted to pretend he didn't hear and took her hand, led her further on to a man-made pond.

In an attempt to cure his boredom the past few days he explored the property and found the place. It proved a relaxing location. He hoped she'd think so too. They sat in the grass a little way from the edge.

"It's beautiful, Chase. Did you plan on bringing me here the whole time?"

Clever woman.

"I thought it would be relaxing."

She nodded, lips quirking in a sexy grin. They sat a while, watching the playful ducks splash about. Eventually she leaned back into the grass and he peered at her. Being a bit odd, he didn't do well with boredom.

"Want to see a trick?"

"Sure. What is it?"

"If you lie flat on your back and bend your knees up, they can support my full weight." He couldn't remember her laughing so hard.

"What?"

"You already told me that before. Remember?"

He shook his head.

"No, when?" She smiled brightly.

"When we were younger, at your house. We were in the hallway by your room, and Roxy too. Tested it out and everything. Wasn't that the same day we dared you to...?"

"Let's never speak of it!" He cut in.

The incident slowly tricked in his memory and he definitely didn't want to remember that particular truth or dare game. He couldn't believe they'd conned him into doing that. Bad things happen when you choose dare with two teenage girls.

"If it makes you feel any better, if not for your being with Roxy, I'd have licked it off." She covered her mouth, turning a deep shade or red. Obviously those words weren't meant to slip.

"Sorry."

How did she know they'd been dating? He'd wanted it kept secret. Her countenance changed as if the memory killed her. It hadn't been a big deal and only lasted a couple of weeks. He never pegged her as the jealous type. Why did it matter? Once more he opted to act like he hadn't heard.

"You would have, huh? What if we play right now?" Her skin burned brighter.

"Isn't that game only for groups of younger people?"

"Oh, I don't know. Why don't we do it, just the two of us? Right now." She leaned on her forearms, former thoughts seemingly forgotten.

"But there's nothing to do here. What are you going to do, dare me to swim with the ducks?"

"You could swim naked." She glared daggers.

"You first."

"How about I dare you to dance for me." The idea clearly terrified her.

"What?"

"I double dare you. You don't have to strip, just dance as sexy as you can." She let out an audible groan of disdain.

"There's no music."

"I'll get the laptop. Another thing. I pick the song."

"Oh God." She mumbled. "You're going to start being a real dick, aren't you?" He chuckled.

"Yep."

She huffed in disapproval.

"Just hurry up, before I change my mind."

With a tilt of his head he started on his way.

"I can't believe I let you talk me into this." He heard her mutter behind him. This would be fun. A million times better than sitting around bored to death, waiting for shit to hit the fan.

Chapter Thirteen

Cassidy

A whirlwind of thoughts flew through her mind as she awaited Chase's return. He actually asked her out. What planet was she on again? Then her slip up concerning Roxy. She face-palmed. If only her mouth had some kind of delay setting.

She remembered that time well. Roxy used to be her best friend, until the betrayal. There were things she perceived as unwritten rules, but vocalized them anyway. Roxy and Rita, her other best friend at the time, both knew what she felt for Chase. She only asked that they tell her if they intended on going out with him, that's all.

Given the hell she endured from home, trust was all the more important to her. Only Rita had any idea from witnessing two of the innumerable incidents she dealt with, so she didn't deal too harshly with Roxy, but they couldn't be friends again.

Whatever went through Chase's mind at the time wasn't what bothered her, he's a guy after all. It was how Roxy had hidden the fact they were together until he left her. That night they played that game, Chase and Roxy took off down the hall every so often, ten minutes at a time, leaving her alone on the couch. She didn't go looking, instinct told what was going on, and shame on her supposed best friend for treating her like an idiot. She believed in BFF etiquette, and Roxy just threw it out the window.

"I'm back." His voice pulled her from her thoughts. He sat, propped the laptop on his lap, and started it up.

"You really expect me to do that?" His response was a cheeky grin.

Seconds later the familiar intro to 'Partition' came on. Anxiety washed over her. This surely amounted to torture. She hesitated.

"What are you waiting for? Get dancing!"

She did her best, refusing to meet his gaze, pulling out every seductive move learned from every instructional video and class, as well as multiple music videos. Her body movements synced with every beat and tempo change. The heat of embarrassment seared every inch of her, and she heaved a sigh of relief once it finished. He muttered something she didn't get as she rushed to sit.

"Your turn." She managed. "Truth or dare."

"Truth." She glared, ignoring the thick, heavy tone.

"Are you serious? After that, you pick truth." He shrugged, eyes full of dark mischief.

"What can I say? Can't top that." She growled in frustration.

"Fine. Umm..." His roaming eyes proved a distraction.

"Why not ask what I'm thinking?"

"It's supposed to be a question that's difficult to answer. If you're willing to tell, it doesn't count." Her mind raced for an idea. "I got it. Have you ever measured your... you know?" He roared, clutching his ribs.

"Yeah." Not the expected answer. She cringed. He laughed again.

"You want to know the size?"

"Nope!" A blush crept in her cheeks as she answered quickly. She really didn't care to find out, nor appreciated how he found her reaction so amusing.

"Your turn."

"Truth."

"What, no dare?"

"Not liking these dares you're choosing." The cocky look that spread across his face had her wanting to slap him.

"OK. I'm setting a limit. At least one dare per two truth." She sighed in resignation.

"Fine."

The mischief in his eyes sent flutters to her stomach.

"So how many guys have you slept with?"

Her eyes bugged out of her head. Was he serious?

"That's a bit of a personal question, don't you think?"

"This is truth or dare, and didn't you ask me if I've ever measured my dick?" She cringed.

As much as she hated to admit it, he had a point. She raised her arms in defeat.

"OK, OK! Four." She didn't understand why he looked so surprised.

"That's it?" Brows furrowed in confusion.

"Yeah. I'm more into the long-term thing and don't do one night stands or flings. I'd rather just take care of things myself."

"Well that saves me from having to ask another question." A groan escaped her as she rolled her eyes.

"Your turn. Truth or dare." He appeared to consider his options.

"Truth." She shook her head. "By your own rules you have to do a dare next time." He grinned.

"Yeah, I know."

This all seemed childish, but it killed boredom, at least for a little while. Perhaps that's why he conned her into doing this. Nothing like a little cabin fever to make a person do crazy things.

"OK. When did you last wet the bed?"

"Not sure, five probably."

"OK. Truth."

"Who or what did you think about the last time you 'took care of things yourself'?" Every inch of her turned every shade of red.

"Gee, it's getting close to supper time..." A cocky grin formed on his face.

"Oh no, you have to tell me. I won't let you leave until you do." Curse him and those wretched eyes.

"You..." She murmured, incapable of looking at him.

"What? I didn't catch that."

"I said you..." At first he looked stunned.

She could almost see his ego inflating to monolithic proportions.

"Wow." He managed after a few seconds. "I've never been part of a woman's wet dream before."

"Yeah, well... Don't let it go to your head."

It appeared a little late for that.

"What was I doing?" Oh no...

"Hey! You already asked your question, and now you have to do a dare!"

"Anything you want." His tone melted her insides.

She looked him over, his grey shirt and blue jeans didn't hide the muscular structure beneath.

"I dare you to wear your clothes inside out for the rest of the evening, and all day tomorrow."

"That's it?"

"Yep." She smiled wickedly. He started taking off his clothes and she turned away.

"What? You're not going to watch?" Her cheeks burned.

"I'm sure you want your privacy." She heard him shuffling around and fought the temptation to peek.

"I'm done." She turned to see him pull the shirt over his taught torso. A giggle escaped her.

"That looks so goofy."

"I bet." He sat next to her.

"Now for your dare." Her insides trembled nervously.

"This is not how I imaged a first date."

"What would you consider a first date?"

"Not sure... Dinner, a movie... Laser tag..."

"Laser tag sounds fun... but right now I dare you to skinny dip in the pond." No way...

"Are you insane? There might leeches, or duck crap, or half a dozen other gross disgusting things. What's the consequence?"

He thought a moment.

"Kiss me, and not just a peck. Make it memorable." It felt like a hundred gymnasts doing flips in her stomach.

What would he consider memorable?

"OK..."

She sat beside him, leaned in, and kissed. It had to be obvious she was nervous. She pulled away, he followed. His hand sifted through her hair, cradling her head as he gently eased her down. Heat issued from his kisses, flowing through her body, turning it to liquid flame. His touch was beyond anything she imagined as he began his slow exploration. She'd never met anyone that affected her as he did. He seemed every bit in control in this as he did everything else.

Her body's only inclination toward him was to give in, even knowing she shouldn't. Not so soon. Never had she cared so deeply about whether a man considered her good enough. His lips broke away, and she whimpered in protest, and shivered as he kissed and nipped a trail down the side of her neck while one of his hands explored beneath her shirt. Her breath hitched as he cupped a breast and she arched as he rolled the stiff nub at its peak between his fingers.

The sound of a phone going off broke the spell. A curse escaped Chase's lips as he reached for the cell in his pocket. A moment of confusion crossed his face before he realized his pants were inside out. He cursed again.

"Hello!" He stood quickly. "Sorry, Sir."

She bit her lip.

"Yeah, she's right here." He handed her the phone.

"Hello?"

"Cassidy, sorry. Did I wake you?"

Confusion filled her.

"No, why?"

"Your voice sounds off."

She swallowed.

"I'm fine. I gave my report earlier... What's going on?"

"I'm calling to inform you I've released part of your pay to your mother's care. So her bill's paid up."

Her heart exploded with joy. Now she only had to worry about the surgery.

"Thank you so much! It means a lot to me!" She could almost picture the smile in his voice.

"You're welcome. Next time, keep your phone within reach. I've tried calling a few times." Crap... "Sorry, I left it inside." "Don't worry about it. Have a good day, miss Macayla."

"You too." She handed the phone back to Chase.

"What was that about?" Chase didn't need burdened by her problems. She wanted to be worthy of his attention, not pitied. Any weakness brought to light would only hinder that. At least, any more than he'd found out already.

"It's nothing for you to worry about. Mercer helped me with something, that's all."

"I see..." His tone could have froze hell over.

"Chase?" He walked away.

"Someday, you will need to trust me." She frowned.

If you knew the secrets I kept, you'd run away, and I'd never see you again...

She didn't follow. One of many lessons learned long ago. Never approach or pursue an angry man. Not that Chase would ever hit her, but between her father and other things, she'd seen enough anger and raging to know she didn't want to be in the midst of any man's warpath.

If he wanted to talk to her again, he would do so when ready. She hoped... She gathered up the laptop and checked the news. As she scrolled down the page, her blood froze. Fourth article down displayed a picture of a house engulfed in flames. Not just any house, the one in which her and her roommates lived. Her home.

She skimmed the article, brought to tears by what she read. Suspected arson, two bodies. Another picture showing nothing left but a shell and rubble. Was this because she was with Chase, or was this Steve's doing? Or both?

As she scrolled down, she saw Steve's picture with a caption saying he was the last person witnessed at the crime scene before the place went up. Guilt rose like bile in her throat. If only she'd been there, she could have saved them. She could have got them out, or stopped Steve, done something. They didn't need to die!

It took everything she had not to smash the laptop to the ground. Anger and helplessness engulfed her. She was livid. Nearly everything that mattered, including her home, gone. All her worldly possessions save for her car, gone. Tears burst from her eyes, refusing to stop.

Chapter Fourteen

Chase

The sun had set before she came in, and she looked like hell. She didn't even notice him as she walked by. Her eyes appeared empty, distant. He followed, watching her mindlessly move about. She put the laptop on her dresser before going to the bathroom. He went in her room, checked the laptop screen, and his heart shattered.

On the screen flashed an article with a picture of Cassidy's home, swallowed up in flames. He read on. He assumed she owned the house but was wrong. Her roommates died in the blaze. No wonder she looked like hell. She'd just lost two people she cared about and became homeless in one fell swoop.

Then there was whatever she dealt with concerning her mother, and her ex. Still she wouldn't tell him anything. He was getting a taste of her world and it terrified him. She had to be the bravest woman he'd ever met, enduring all these things. Yet she braved it alone.

It was the saddest thing he'd ever seen, and it gnawed at him. The biggest questions running through his mind were... Why couldn't she open up to him? When would she trust him? She shouldn't have to shoulder this alone. He left the room, just reaching the kitchen when she approached.

"Sorry I'm late making supper. I'll get started on some spaghetti." He blinked in disbelief.

She went on as if nothing happened. If it were him, he wouldn't want to do anything but drink. What kind of coping mechanisms did she have? He wanted to ask about it but she probably wouldn't tell him anything anyhow. If he mentioned the article, she'd realize he'd been in her room.

"Sure, spaghetti would be nice. Would you like some help?" She shook her head.

"No, thank you. It's my job, remember? You just take care of yourself. I can manage." No doubt what little of the difficulties she allowed him to discover, so much more lay hidden.

He still didn't understand why she opened up more with the Sergeant Major than with him. The measure of pain that caused him was immeasurable.

"Cassidy, is there anything you want to talk about? Something bothering you?" She put on a bright smile, but at this point he was quickly learning many of them were fake.

How many years had she been practising that smile? The wall he recognized came up once again.

"Nothing you need to worry about. I'm fine."

"Cassidy..." The growl came out harsher than intended. She wrung her fingers together.

"Is there anything else you want with the spaghetti? I can make chicken parmigiana, or meatballs. I can also make a superb chocolate bean cake." Frustration simmered in his veins.

"So this is how it is then? You want to play games?" Her eyes shot wide open.

"What? No!"

"Then what's wrong?" She trembled, eyes glassy.

"Look, Chase! If I have any problems, they're mine. I'm sure there are things you don't tell me. I don't want anyone's pity, especially yours! The last thing I need is for you to treat me like some kind of... of charity case!" She threw her arms in the air.

"Then the next thing I know you'll take off once this is all over, and I'll never see or hear from you again. That would..." With a roar of frustration she ran to her room and slammed the door.

No mistaking the tears in her eyes. The words she didn't speak screamed loudest. His opinion mattered to her, he mattered to her, and the idea of never seeing him again seemed most painful. She hid such tremendous fear. She feared he'd abandon her, that he'd see her as nothing more than some pitiful creature and that he didn't truly care.

None of that could be further from the truth, but he was helpless to get her to trust him, she had to come to it on her own. At least now he received a bit more understanding, along with a whole new set of questions. One was most prevalent. What made her this way in the first place?

For the first time in months he ate cereal for supper. Not the greatest meal in the world, especially after eating anything Cassidy made, but he didn't dare approach her. He couldn't help feeling like a bit of an ass, pushing her like that, but it yielded some information. She had a tough shell to crack, but he enjoyed a challenge.

He awoke to the sound of Cassidy's ringing phone. On the way to the bathroom, rubbing the sleep from his eyes, he heard her yell. He pulled his cell from his inside-out pocket. Almost noon. He approached her door. He was about to knock when her distressed voice carried through the door.

"A stroke? What do you mean? You're supposed to be professionals! That surgery was meant to save her life!" A moment of silence. "N–no! The last thing I need right now is 'sorry'!" A growl of frustration followed, and the phone rang again.

"Hello!" A pause. "Yes, I saw the pictures and read about your handiwork, *Steve*. I swear, if the cops don't catch you for what you did I'll kill you myself! Don't you ever–EVER fucking call me again!" A shriek rang out, followed by a loud crash as something hit the wall close to him.

This was not the calm, cool and collected Cassidy he'd known all these years. This was a woman grasping for one last ounce of sanity after losing everything. He shouldn't barge in, but he couldn't just leave her like this. Knowing she was in so much pain killed him.

"Cassidy?" He saw the remnants of a beer bottle splayed across the floor before the wall, an indent where it hit. Cassidy lay sprawled across the bed in tears. He rushed to her side.

"Cassidy, what's wrong?" She shrugged him off. "I don't need your pity!" She sobbed.

It took everything to exercise patience. Perhaps he'd finally met someone who's stubbornness truly rivalled his own.

"I'm not here to pity you. I want to be here for you. What do you need?"

"You're not supposed to see me like this, Chase. I'm supposed to be brave, strong, like you, not weak." He rubbed her back, stunned at this revelation.

"You are brave, one of the bravest people I've met. Everyone has their moment of weakness, no matter who they are. You don't need to take on the world by yourself." She snickered.

"It's easy for you to say. You don't really know much about me." He stared, bewildered.

What did he need to know? She was a kind person. Beautiful. Smart. Considerate. A great cook. And able to dance just as sexy as a well choreographed pop star.

"Why don't you enlighten me?" She shook her head, a fat tear rolling down her cheek.

"You'll just run away, then it'll be another fifteen to twenty years before I see you again, if I'm lucky." He let out an exasperated sigh.

"You need to trust me, we have to communicate, or nothing can work out." She sat up, he wrapped an arm around her. She leaned against him.

"I want to... You're such an amazing person Chase. I don't want to be a burden to you, I want to be deserving of your respect, and I don't want to tarnish any positive image you have of me." What could she have ever done that would make that happen?

He got something, that had to be enough for now. Any more prying would likely drive her away, and that wall would come up once again. Everything with her needed done one step at a time.

"Alright. Will you at least tell me why you're upset? I won't think less of you, I promise."

"Thank you, but there's nothing you can do to fix things."

"Talking about what's bothering you doesn't make you weak, and I don't consider it a burden." She seemed to consider his words. "Please." At first it didn't seem she'd say anything.

He held his tongue and bid on patience.

"My mother got run over by a drunk driver months back. She'd been in a coma ever since, and I found out recently that she developed an aneurysm. They operated on her today but during the operation she suffered a stroke... She didn't make it." He waited, held her tighter, kissed her gently on the forehead.

"My ex won't leave me alone either. He set fire to my home. My roommates, my best friends... didn't make it. He did it as they slept, knowing they were there, to get back at me for leaving him." He did his best to mask his emotions, but inside he raged.

Who the hell would ever assume that kind of thing to be OK? Not feeling sorry for her when it seemed life dealt her one bad hand after another was impossible.

"Is there anything you want me to do? Can I help in any way?" She shook her head.

"No, you don't need to be my hero, coming in and trying to fix things."

"I want to help."

"If you really want to help me, just be there. Bad enough buying me dinner." It was a hard pill to swallow, but he understood. She'd rather give than a receive and relying on others was hard to deal with.

"You don't owe me anything Cassidy. I wanted to do it. I'll try to honour your request, but don't shut me out like you've been doing."

"It's hard."

He wrapped his arms around her, lightly squeezing her trembling frame. Despite how hard he tried to ignore it, the floral scent wafting from her, and her soft skin left him wanting to do things far too inappropriate given the circumstances. At least now she wasn't trying to send him away. "It's OK, Cassidy. I'm here if you need me." He sensed doubt radiating off her in waves.

She didn't utter a word as she leaned into him, tears staining his shirt as she sobbed against him. He gently rubbed circles over her back, sometimes petting her hair, offering whatever comfort possible. He'd made some progress. She'd taken a leap of faith in trusting him. He only hoped he wouldn't screw up and send her right back into her shell.

When it came to womens' emotions and tears, he was uncomfortable and completely out of his element. That's on a regular basis. A distraught Cassidy was a whole different level.

Days passed and even though she was miserable, she tried to act like everything wasn't falling apart. He leaned against the wall, watching her lay into the punching bag like it was the source of all her problems.

"Keep going like that and you'll send it flying into next week." She offered the usual well practised smile he recognized and wiped at the sweat dripping from her forehead with the back of a wrapped hand.

"If that's the case, I'll have to buy it a passport." At least her humour was intact.

It surprised him she didn't drink herself into a stupor. He probably would.

"Would you like to join me for a picnic?" She eyed him in confusion.

"Am I late making lunch? I must have lost track of time, sorry." He shook his head.

"No, but I wonder if you'd like one out back, and relax a little."

OK, so he couldn't cook worth a damn. A cold plate of sandwiches and other finger foods were better than nothing. His leg was much better, and he'd stopped using the cane, and the bruising on his ribs had greatly dissipated, so doing things around the place was much easier. Yet she still insisted on trying to take care of everything.

It appeared she was trying to escape into her job. He hated seeing her this way. As she turned, the dark circles under her eyes became apparent. He shook his head. All this overexertion was likely to kill her.

It reminded him of when he was younger, seeing his mother after a long week of overtime just trying to keep them afloat. It ripped at his heart.

"Just let me get cleaned up and I'll join you." He nodded.

"Sure."

As she passed he noticed just how gaunt she'd become, but she was still beautiful. He hoped she'd take it easy. As he watched the natural sway of her hips, thoughts of giving her his brand of release flooded him. He gritted his teeth. It was not the time to be eyeing her like candy. For the problems he was dealing with, hers ran just as deep.

She was quiet as they ate, leaning back over lush green grass overlooking the pond. She nibbled on a celery stick, staring up thoughtfully. Her expression, mournful. He was at a loss what to say so he poured some champagne into a couple of flute glasses, handing one to her. She turned, smiled, accepting appreciatively. He couldn't help the way his body reacted to how her knee length, silken dress played off her curves.

"Thank you."

He moved closer to her as she spoke.

"You look... stunning." He managed after a moment.

A blush crept into her cheeks. The first sign of life in her he'd seen in days. She gave a coy smile.

"Thank you. Again." She tipped the glass against her lips, taking a small sip.

"Perhaps when we're done here, we might get a place together?." Why did he just blurt that out?

It wasn't like him to speak so thoughtlessly, or move things so fast. He'd always been one to plan out everything, fifty steps ahead. Her eyes bugged out in surprise before the wheels in her head turned.

"What do you mean? As roommates?" That look told him it was the only acceptable circumstance to which she might concede. He took a gulp from his glass before speaking.

"Yes, of course." She gently swirled the liquid in her glass as she stared into it, biting her lip pensively.

"I'll consider it." He was grateful her mind was working clearer than his at the moment. He needed to change the subject, fast.

It felt like he was riding the Titanic.

"So how's your father taking all this? Is he going to hold off on things until you can go to the..." His voice trailed off as her hands visibly tightened around the glass. He swore he heard it crack. She swallowed.

"My father died... a long time ago. My brother is all I have left, and he's neck deep in drugs. So I'm on my own in this." His heart sank.

"I'm sorry." He murmured.

She peered up, her glassy eyes straining to focus as she gave a sad smile. Her expression shredded his heart.

"Don't be sorry, Chase. He and I were never close, and my brother chose that path. Only he can get himself off." She studied his face for a moment before picking out a cucumber slice from a container beside the large basket.

"Thank you for this picnic, Chase. It was very considerate of you." All her troubles and here she was, worrying about his feelings. It tugged at his heart.

He watched as she nibbled on the vegetable, wanting to lick the water off her lips. Heat coursed through him.

"You're welcome." She drew closer, leaning on his shoulder, peering up at the near cloudless sky. A warm breeze swept past, and she shivered against him, her loose silken strands caressing his face. She turned to him, placing a chaste kiss on his cheek.

He went to wrap his arm around her when a tingling sensation shot from his shoulder to his fingers. He pumped his hand against it. Electric currents buzzed in his head and a pungent smell, like burnt rubber, filled his nostrils. His vision blurred.

Cassidy must have sensed something as she looked at him because her expression turned frantic.

"Chase? What's wrong?" He struggled to speak but to his own ears his words were a garbled mess. She backed up slightly, shaking.

"Chase?" He fell to his side, the world around him turning dark.

Panic struck. Every muscle tensed. The last thing he heard was a terrified Cassidy screaming his name, tears apparent in her voice, before his mind fell into darkness.

Pain seared every inch, every muscle burned. There was a vile sensation in his mouth and nausea threatened another dose. Quiet sobs graced his ears. Where was he, and why did it feel like he just got worked over like a POW being pumped for information?

He forced his eyes open as a cascade of images flashed through his mind. Driving, an explosion, men yelling, shots fired, it was so much, too much. A fresh dose of pain exploded in his head. He put a hand to his head with a groan. Why was he on his side? As he slowly sat up, he winced at the remnants of his stomach contents on the ground. It took a moment to realize where he was. He couldn't understand what happened, why Cassidy looked so upset, or why his shirt was partially unbuttoned or his pants undone.

"Ch-Chase?"

"What happened?" Relief crept in her features and she approached cautiously.

"You... you had a seizure." He sensed it may have been her first time seeing one.

"Why are my clothes undone?" Had she been trembling like that the entire time? How long had he been out?

"In my training we're taught to loosen tight clothing so that nothing restricts your movement. I had to put you back on your side because you choked on your own vomit." A rush of embarrassment sped through him.

Knowing a seizure was inevitable didn't make things any better.

"I had to let Mercer know. He told me not to worry..." He could see how well that worked by her tear stained face, every trembling limb, every swallow, and the paleness of her skin... She looked terrified.

Usually his ego, his pride would get the better of him, but her gentle tone, and the fragility she portrayed, ripped the air from his lungs and bled his heart. It brought forth his need to protect unlike anything he'd ever known.

Her chest heaved as another sob escaped her. You'd think he was dying or something. After she lost so much already, it was hard not to feel for her.

"Cassidy, I'm alright, really. You don't need to cry." She wiped away a tear.

"I know, but it scared the hell out of me. You sure you're OK?" He smiled and inched closer, the soreness and pain only slightly better.

"Do you think you can walk?" He backed slightly, scanning her face.

Worry seeped from every feature.

"Yeah."

"Perhaps you should get washed up and relax, maybe lie down for a while. Take a nap. When you're ready, Mercer would like to know if you remember anything." He groaned.

He may have recalled much of the events surrounding the explosion, but not where he'd hidden the information.

"T-take your time, though. Don't want you to get sick again or anything like that again." Judging from the look on her face, she'd be worrying about this for a long time. He sighed.

"Alright. I can't wait to get out of these clothes anyway." He watched as she gathered up their food and shoved it all in the basket.

"How long have I been out?"

"Five minutes, roughly. After it finished you were out cold for a long time. I had to check on you a few times to make sure you're still breathing." She flipped the lid closed after putting in the bottle of champagne and lifted the basket as she stood.

"I don't like this, Chase. If I wasn't around..." She swallowed against the anxiety and fear that emanated from her.

"Please, please be careful!"

"It'll be alright. You don't need to worry about me." Doubt was evident, but he said nothing more, and she didn't argue.

He thought nothing would help ease her anxiety but time. What a swell plan this turned out to be. He determined to make it up to her.

Come evening, he was showered, shaved, and a bit more lively. The muscle soreness had dissipated immensely, and though the pull of fatigue was strong, he wanted to make up for the ruined picnic. It troubled him how he'd gone out trying to ease her pain, only to cause her more.

His stomach rumbled as the aromatic blending of spiced meat and herbs teased his nostrils. He sat straighter and watched as Cassidy approached, setting a steaming bowl on the table before him. He peered down at the contents. Chicken, carrots, celery, onions, and potatoes. Hurriedly he picked up his spoon and dug in. The flavours burst in his mouth, like heaven.

"It's delicious, thank you." He said after swallowing.

Colour tinged her cheeks.

"I'm glad you like it." She sat next to him after retrieving her own bowl.

He nudged his seat closer. Cassidy watch curiously. Just how would he make it up to her?

"So you still like dancing?" Not his favourite activity, but he didn't outright hate it either.

"Yeah, but I don't do ballroom dancing. Never learned. But I've learned some belly dancing, and after a while I can imitate what I see in music videos. I used to have a dance pole too, but didn't get too far learning how to use it." A hint of shyness adorned her features.

"Few people knew of that though. My mother told me I have a natural talent. She liked dancing too. But not pole dancing, she never did that. I think she'd have killed me if she ever found out." Her eyes became sorrowful and guilt clawed at him for putting that look on her face.

It warred against the heat searing his blood imagining seeing her at the pole. Words failed him. She basically just told him she had a wilder side than she let on. What had she gotten into since they stopped talking? He took another spoonful of soup.

"Do you?"

"It's alright. Not my favourite, but I don't mind. But never poled danced, not something that'd interest me." A slight grin touched her lips. "Thought maybe you'd like to find some music afterwards, and we could dance." For a moment her eyes lit up and those green emeralds shone every bit like the gem, but quickly lost their lustre.

"I don't think it's a good idea. You should rest, get some sleep soon. I don't want anything to happen to you and..."

"You're afraid something will happen to me?" She nodded, her lips pressed in a grim line.

"Is there anything I can do to make things at least a little better?" Her expression was of astonishment.

Had anyone ever inquired about her wants and needs before?

"Just... take care of yourself. Don't wear yourself out. Please. I'd hate for something to happen to you." He wondered if she fretted like this when he told her he wanted to join the army.

It bothered him to think so.

"Alright. How about tomorrow?" She offered a slight smile.

"If you want to, sure." They continued eating for a while in silence.

He wasn't sure what else to say for the longest time. She still bore a look of concern on her face, and her complexion was still pale, though not as much as when the seizure struck him. It was Cassidy who broke the silence.

"Do you think you'll ever retire from... whatever it is you're doing? What exactly are you? I mean, you're a special agent but you have a military commanding officer. I'm confused."

He weighed his words. Saying too much could be hazardous. Not that they weren't in a precarious situation already.

"I'm trained for more than one position and am called upon to jump from one to another from time to time. That's all I can say."

She nodded in acknowledgement but didn't push.

I don't know when I'll leave, either. She looked down at her bowl, likely to hide her expression, but he could see it wasn't the answer she wanted.

"Oh, OK."

Would that be a deal breaker? She'd said yes to being with him, but she'd never dealt with separation for an extended period on account of his work. He should have considered that before asking. He still struggled with words when she changed the subject.

"Do you like to cook?" He shook his head. Any time he tried, the result usually ended the same. Something akin to charcoal.

"No. It's not a skill I possess." Another bout of silence.

"Do you remember anything?" He'd told the Sergeant Major what little he remembered, but the grizzly memories she didn't need to hear. Just one more thing to add to the pile for her to worry about.

"Bits and pieces, not much." She wasn't sure whether to believe him. Once again, she changed the subject.

"After this, would you like to try some of my chocolate bean cake?"

He eyed her quizzically. It didn't sound too appetizing. She seemed to read his mind.

"It's not gross, I promise. You can't even taste the beans. And it's low carb. Judging by what's in the cupboards, Mercer's a real health nut, but I'm not complaining." She let out a melodic giggle, smiling brightly.

Did anyone ever say 'no' to her? The glint in her eyes and that crook of a smile, she was sexy, and she didn't even know. If he didn't like it, he didn't have to eat it ever again.

What would it hurt to try it?

"I'll give it a shot, sure." Her eyes lit up, and she nipped her lower lip.

"Thank you!"

He resisted the urge to pounce on her. She would likely worry about him overexerting himself. That was the last thing he needed.

It wasn't long after eating before he retired for the night. Unable to keep his eyes open, he drifted into a surreal place where he could explore every part of Cassidy he hadn't seen.

Chapter Fifteen

Cassidy

Cassidy stood before the large vanity mirror, staring at her reflection. Thoughts like voices at war in her mind. As though her heart fought against the voices of her parents, and her demons. There was no question what lay in her heart, but anxiety was relentless. What he instilled in her went beyond understanding. Despite trying so hard to ignore it, fight it, for her own sake, her own safety, it won over.

The mirror reflected nothing but ugliness. She was nothing more than a fool.

Should I tell him?

Don't do it Cassidy...

Is it worth the risk?

He will reject you. Look at you! You're ugly, fat, worthless... You've got nothing going for you, he's way out of your league. You're crazy for even thinking about him, wanting him that way. Haven't your parents taught you anything? If you do this, what would your father say if he found out? What would he do? You really want to take that risk? You must be the biggest idiot on the planet to even be considering this!

No one's ever gotten to me like this before. He's unlike any guy I've ever met. Even if he rejects me, even if my parents are right, at least he'll realize he's an amazing person. Surely he'll get that it's because of who he is, not just what he looks like. There are many good-looking guys in the world, but none of them have the character or a mind like Chase.

You have to be the biggest idiot, and the craziest person on the planet. You deserve what pain and suffering you'll get.

In the cool of the summer evening she stood there at the park, close by the monkey bars. Probably the safest place since her parents were home, out of sight, out of earshot. How the hell did she get him alone? Her palms sweat. Her heart raced. She bit her lip, swallowed at the lump in her throat. Even though she'd planned it out in her head, it didn't stop the anxiety from taking over, from turning her mind to mush. How did he gain mastery over her, beyond that of the demons that haunted her?

"Chase, there's something I want to tell you."

You're not seriously doing this! Haven't your parents taught you anything? You're not good enough for him! You're not good enough for anybody. This is a foolish waste of time! He's light-years out of your league. Abort mission! ABORT!

He scanned her, curious. Terror filled her. Her heart threatened to break from her chest. She really shouldn't do this. To give him her heart meant he'd have power over her, power to break that heart, to hurt her worse than her father ever did.

Did she want to give him that power? Looking at him, the intelligence in his eyes, mixed with something else... something akin to a siren's song.

"What is it, Cassidy?"

Her breath quickened and the world around her darkened until only he remained. Her body trembled uncontrollably. She risked their friendship. He'd call her a fool. Laugh at her. Ridicule her. Her parents were right. There's no way they weren't. She cast her eyes to the ground, afraid. His value rested so far above hers it frightened her. She wrung her fingers nervously.

Maybe... maybe he'd see something in her, hold something in his heart for her. Perhaps he'd care about her personality more than her looks. He was everything she wasn't, all the things she lacked, the most wonderful person she'd ever met...

"I-I love you." How she didn't pass out was beyond comprehension. A moment of silence. She stood on the precipice of blacking out completely.

"Cassidy, look at me. Look in my eyes and say it." Her breath halted. His voice was gentle. Was there a chance? But how could he doubt her? Just because she wasn't looking at him? Did he not understand fear? The possible negative consequences for her? If her father found out...

If this was an out, she wasn't taking it. And if her father found out, she'd deal with it. Frustration surfaced, and she looked in his eyes and said it again, searching for the purpose of his request.

"I love you." She couldn't breathe. He seemed to understand her unvoiced question.

"You can tell if someone loves you when you look in their eyes." Her heart shattered.

Not only did he reject her, he didn't even believe she meant it. She was at a loss for words. After fighting her fear, her anxiety, and every negative thing her parents instilled in her to give him her heart, risking the cruel hand of her father, he didn't even believe her genuine. There remained no worse thing he could have done to her. But he had no idea the hell she lived in because she never told him.

Because of that, and only that, she found it impossible to even be angry with him. She scrambled for some form of coherent speech. She would have taken a punch to the face over that answer. Either a reciprocation, a 'sorry, I don't feel that way, but I appreciate your bravery', or a punch to the face. At least if he punched hard enough, it might make her forget it ever happened, or knock some sense into her.

"Oh, OK." It was all her voice would allow.

She refused to cry. He would never see her weak. He was wrong. From her upbringing she'd learned the only real way to tell if someone loves you. By their actions. Yes, his was a romantic notion, but she'd seen her parents profess their 'love' while looking in each other's eyes. She'd also seen her father literally bust through a door to beat her mother. So clearly, it was a gesture that bore little meaning.

Her parents were right. Right about how horrible she was. About everything. She wished there was a hole for her to crawl in where she might forget everything. That was impossible, and she needed to accept the truth of what it was, who she was, what she'd known all along. But there would be no one like Chase, her Achilles heel which she was helpless to do anything about.

This was her epiphany. That she'd taken the path of Icarus. Flown too close to the sun. Now all that remained was to rise from the ashes and pray there were enough pieces of her left to pick up.

Cassidy awoke in a cold sweat. The dream, it was a memory, and she remembered everything. She wanted to cry. She knew what brought it on. The day before, watching as Chase thrashed about, choking, spewing.

It eluded her how she'd been able to move. Turning him to his side and undoing his shirt buttons, along with the belt at his waist and the zipper of his jeans. All she understood was terror. Everything turned cold as blood rushed away from her face and shaky hands. Her mind had been on autopilot. Yet she still remembered what she said.

He'd been too far gone to hear her, but the memories of the moment in the park bore down on her like a freight train. Mowed her down painfully and dragged her through mental and emotional hell. In keeping silent, her dream made sure she didn't forget.

What a fool she'd been. A complete idiot. She should have kept her mouth shut and spared herself the heart-ache and embarrassment that followed her through the rest of her life. Until now.

Cassidy jumped out of bed. A relaxing bubble bath was tempting. Given all the frustration and anxiety of late, and then what happened yesterday, it amazed her she hadn't just said 'to hell with this' and drowned herself in the pond.

After throwing on a white tank top and blue jeans she grabbed a towel and headed to the bathroom. Half-way there, a slow melody flooded the hallway. A familiar song, a distant memory, hazy as a dream.

Her breath caught in her throat and she turned. Her heart swelled. That was years ago, around the same time she'd foolishly confessed her feelings. Only, she'd sung it on a dare. Did he remember her confession? Just how much about that time did he remember?

"I was wondering when you'd get up." He leaned against the wall, arms crossed, wearing a black T-shirt and blue jeans, looking every bit a like man bent on conquest. A corner of his mouth crooked up, his eyes shone like polished blue topaz. They burned a trail of liquid fire over every inch of her.

"I thought for sure you'd be sleeping in after what happened."

"I owe you for ruining our picnic." He tilted his head curtly. "Come, dance." She approached, stomach in knots.

Hopefully he wouldn't over do it today. Guilt still clawed at her insides, left her wondering if she was to blame for it. A contributing factor at least.

"Oh Chase, you shouldn't blame yourself! That hardly seems fair. You didn't need to do that anyway. Thank you, it was thoughtful."

He wrapped his arms around her.

"It *was* my fault." He pressed his lips against hers with a gentle pressure. She leaned in, but he backed away, pulling her toward him. She shook her head at his words.

Reaching the centre of the living room, he ran to the computer, restarting the song. She tossed the towel on the nearby chair. Soon he took her in his arms, pressed her tight against him, and she let her forearms gently fall over his shoulders. Her hands rested against the nape of his neck. Should she let on she remembered the song, or was that just one more thing better buried in the past?

His body heat seeped through their fabric, scorching her. It was impossible to ignore the fear that the clock was ticking on their time together, and she wished this moment could last forever. Perhaps the dream was an omen. If so, a bad one. At least he hadn't been as short with her since finding out about her difficulties.

It was so strange, with all his problems, he insisted on thinking of her. It was sweet, and surprising. Another mystery to her. Something she'd never encountered with any other man. Just one more thing to remind her that any woman would be lucky to have him. And for once, luck favoured her... For the time being.

"I assume you slept well." She teased.

"Like a log." A soft chuckle escaped her at the way he responded.

"How are you doing now?"

"Better. The bruises are gone and my leg's almost like new."

She rested her cheek against his chest. His heart drummed a steady, soothing rhythm against her ear as they turned slowly.

"I wish this would last forever." She sighed against him. A hand caressed her cheek, fingers ran through her hair. She lifted her head.

"You're not a bad dancer." His expression screamed disbelief.

"And what do you consider bad dancing?"

"Stepping on my feet."

He laughed.

"Such low expectations." She smiled.

"I guess that depends on how you see things."

"Have you always held such low expectations?" She shook her head.

"Not always. You surpass all mine by leaps and bounds." He let out a heartier laugh.

"I am perfect, aren't I?" Now it was her turn, with a playful slap on his chest.

"I wouldn't say that. But by all means, keep trying." Once again she leaned her head against his chest, crooked beneath his chin.

The song neared completion when Chases' cell phone rang. Her heart sank.

Why couldn't the caller have waited?

"Hello?... Yes Sir." She backed away, picked up her towel, and started toward the bathroom. His face looked grim, and she wasn't sure if she should ask.

Ignoring the drumming in her chest she walked past him. She wanted to stay, but the dream was still fresh in her mind and one perfect moment wouldn't erase the anxiety. There was no shaking the notion she was playing the fool all over again. That just like back then, this would all crash and burn.

"When was the information released?" It was the last thing she heard before closing the door and hopping in the tub.

She cranked the water as hot as she could stand and sank into it, hoping to clear her mind and rid herself of the sense that things were about to take a turn for the worse.

"Steve got caught." Cassidy jumped as she opened the door to the bathroom. There Chase stood, expression inscrutable. How long had he been standing there?

"What?" She straightened her shirt.

"Steve, your ex. He got arrested late last night." A sigh of relief escaped her.

"Will they charge him with anything?" Only the faintest twitch of his lips was obvious.

"Yeah. They have enough to pin him for arson and two counts of murder."

She sensed there was more and quietly waited.

"There's also a problem." She tried to tamp down the dread threatening to overwhelm her. Instinct told her it involved the people who wanted Chase, and what knowledge he possessed. She nodded for him to continue. "Seems our defector figured out our bodies weren't at the scene. It's not definite yet, but they may have found out where we are."

Her eyes widened, bewildered.

"How? Doesn't he keep that information hush-hush?" He nodded.

"Yes, but you can't hide satellite imagery, and the traitor has a hacker working with him. Someone hacked into Mercer's personal computer and got a fair bit of info before he could stop it. They're still trying to figure it all out."

She was at a loss for what to think, say, do, for the longest time.

"Then they know we're here? Did they get any army intelligence stuff? Why'd they target him?" His expression became quizzical before he chuckled. She felt every inch an idiot.

"No, he doesn't keep 'army intelligence stuff' on his personal computer. But plans for this place, information on his family, that kind of thing, yeah. The traitor knows I report to him, probably wanted to see if there was anything about me on his computer, since anything in the office is about a secure as Fort Knox."

This was bad...

"He's in trouble?" A cold sweat started at her brow.

"Not really, and there's nothing on there about me."

"What about his family?"

"They're being taken care of."

The danger she wished so badly to avoid was closing in faster than expected. His enemy clearly didn't like to waste time. A suffocating hedge of fear and foreboding closed in, warning of her inevitable death. This would likely be the last bit of time she had left with Chase. The knowledge tied her up in knots. Chase framed her face with his hands. Would he get his memory back before the enemy arrived, or just in time for it to be too late?

He was hiding something, but she didn't want to push, fearing she wouldn't like what she'd hear.

"It'll be alright. We'll be fine." The uncertainty that flashed in his eyes didn't escape her.

He was trying to appease her, calm her down. It didn't work. She shrugged away as he tried to hold her. Resisted the warmth and strength he offered, the virile energy he exuded that threatened to draw her in, make her forget herself.

She didn't want to be lied to, coddled, sheltered and protected like a helpless child. She never had it growing up, pointless to start now. All she wanted was the truth. Perhaps it was cold, sometimes life was. Cold, ruthless, unforgiving.

"Don't... Don't ever lie to me." Concern and pity poured from his features.

"OK... We'll stay alive, or die trying." Such a peculiar thing to say, but she got what he was trying for. She tilted the corner of her mouth in a half smile.

"Right."

He took in the sight of her, his eyes reflected molten pools.

"Come, let me make you forget. At least, for a little while..." A tremor rocketed through her spine at the deep, silken edge in his voice. An unspoken promise her body understood. Her mind screamed for her to wait. If she did this, and he found out about her past, and took off, it would kill her.

"Oh Chase, you know I'm only interested in doing something if it's serious."

He wrapped his arms around her.

"I'm not going anywhere. I mean it." He pressed his lips gently against hers.

She could trust him, right? As his mouth became ravenous, her mind went blank, lost in a wave of delicious, sweet heat travelling the length of her body, resting at the centre of her hips. As a hand began its gentle caress of her face, neck, shoulders, the way he did it, she could have sworn he'd practised this a million times.

"Come on, we can pretend the rest of the world doesn't exist for the next while. I promise, I'm not playing you. I'd never do that to you. *Never* you, Cassidy." His breath was hot, like a caress across her cheek.

Anxiety crept in. This could be her last, only chance with him. He picked up on her emotion.

"You don't need to worry, I know what I'm good at."

If she'd been capable of thought, it would have given her pause. But only Chase ever possessed the ability to make her lose sense of rationality so completely. And the confident promise ushered in that thick, rich voice, held enough power to do her in.

His mouth was on hers once more, scorching, exploring, she barely noticed as he guided her to his room, his bed. He ripped her shirt over her head, and as he did the same to his own, she leaned over, unzipping his fly with her teeth as she undid the button of his jeans, then slid them down. The evidence of his arousal sprang up, peaking through his boxers. When she looked up, he stared, fixated.

"Thought you said you'd only been with four people."

A coy smile played across her face.

"It's true, but it helps to have a willingness to learn. There's lots of things people don't know about me. Used to tie cherry stems with just tongue and teeth too."

His member pulsed, and he groaned.

"Anything else you want to tell me?"

Her smiled widened devilishly.

"All surprises are earned."

He sprang on her with a low growl, like a voracious predator, eager to conquer its prey. She squealed in surprise. In the blink of an eye, she lay sprawled on the mattress, arms pinned overhead, his mouth crushing hers with all the ferocity and passion he possessed.

"It's not smart to tease wild animals." He managed throatily. Between his mouth, and the branding of a well practised hand roaming her body, igniting every inch of her, she was on fire.

"You're calling yourself a wild animal?" She managed through the haze of her mind. Even to her own ears, her voice sounded unlike her own. Charged, heated, echoing the luscious chaos rampant in her body, which he orchestrated in a way that was uniquely him.

"Woman, you have no idea..." He whispered hoarsely before his mouth, tongue, followed the path seared by his hand. So that sounded a little cheesy, her body didn't care. She shivered.

Was that a hint at his previous exploits and relationships? She never asked how many, didn't want to know. Perhaps that long lineup of women really existed somewhere. She shuddered once more. From the slow grind of his hand against the nub at the apex of her thighs, or the multiple sources from which he drew experience, she couldn't be sure. She really didn't want to share. Those days were far behind her.

She gasped, arched when his mouth captured the hardened peak of a breast, his tongue eliciting a soft moan from her as she clutched the pillow beneath her head. Languid heat pooled below as he widened her legs and slid one finger, then two, into her core, milking the dew from within. Pressure spiralled from her centre as his fingers weaved their magic.

"Fuck, you're tight!" She blushed in spite of herself at his surprise as he pulled his fingers out, giving his hand a shake. "You have to be tighter than a Cheerio! When was the last time you got laid?"

She shrugged. "Umm... It's been a while..." Like he needed to know. She'd always been able to handle things on her own. At first she thought he'd stop, but it only drove him on.

He rose to his feet at the foot of the bed, pulled off his boxers, and the glory previously sheathed, thick, long enough it nearly reached his navel, sprang free. Her eyes consumed every inch of his form, every fluid muscle movement that alluded to the man hidden within, both dangerous and erotic, a modern embodiment of Ares.

He walked over to the small wooden nightstand and pulled something small and plastic from the drawer.

"You always keep condoms with you? A little presumptuous, don't you think?" He chuckled.

"Nah. There was a box mixed in with what he brought me." Her eyes widened in disbelief. When his superior thought of everything, he thought of everything. Cassidy didn't know what to think about that.

He was on her once more, she brushed her fingers over one of the scars splayed across his chest. She didn't want to imagine the pain he must have suffered.

"It only hurt when it happened. Don't worry about it." He ravished her mouth with his, sending her back into sensual oblivion. Her lids fluttered closed as her mouth relinquished a soft moan against his. His hands resumed their exploration, and she writhed beneath his touch.

"You're so fucking beautiful." He breathed.

She managed a breathy giggle.

"Pot, meet kettle." He merely grunted in return.

A moment later the sound of a wrapper tearing graced her ears. In seconds she felt the fullness of him inside and mounting pressure as he laid claim to her body. As she'd always wanted, as it always should have been. She tilted her hips, wrapped her legs around his waist, giving him deeper access. She clutched his shoulders, hands sliding to his biceps, nails digging slightly into his skin.

The deep groans he managed between pants, matching his thrusts, sent tremors throughout, adding to the heat coursing through her. The coil of pleasure soon crested, exploded, her body arching, awash in rapture. He quickly followed, clutching her hips, stiffening, quickening, releasing with a long groan and shuddering of his hips.

Slowly her eyes opened, body spent. He rolled to her side. She gradually caught her breath. Reality made its unwelcome descent. She hoped she hadn't just made a big mistake.

Turning her head, she watched him rest an arm over his head, other across his taut stomach. A part of her felt lucky, like she'd just received a gift from the gods. The other, like this was some grand cosmic joke and he would disappear, like waking from a dream, into a nightmare.

She didn't want to face reality, the inevitable end, the realization that she'd lost everything. To know his warming of her body, this bed, all nothing more than a calm before the storm. Even if they survived the impending disaster, assuming he wanted to stay, he'd want to know more about her. Things that would send him away for good.

Once his breath had calmed, he turned on his side, facing her. He traced a line over the contours of her body with a finger.

"You are a surprise Cassidy." His lips brushed the tip of her nose, feather light, then her forehead.

"So are you." Her hands rested against his chest.

If only it were possible to freeze time. She remembered all too well. Summer days alone with him, knowing she'd have to leave but would have given anything to stay. Watching the sun set and silently praying it would freeze, just for a few more precious moments.

A flash of them in his backyard, the setting sun painting the sky a rich tapestry of pinks and oranges, sitting on the grass, wanting nothing more than to be close to him, but unable to. She'd foolishly dared to fly too close to the sun, and it cost her dearly. But it hadn't stopped her heart from wanting. The last thing they'd talked about that night were earwigs.

Yes, earwigs, stupid little creepy crawly bugs. They gave her the willies, but she didn't care. She'd have listened to him talk about anything if it meant she would hear his beautiful voice, and that she didn't have to go. How young, naïve, and stupid she'd been. What it conjured up inside, being there with him, then gone, indescribable. She lay with him now, but history would only repeat itself.

"Something wrong? You look deep in thought." She inched closer, resting her head against him. She didn't want to burden him with her worries, her insecurities, and didn't want to drum up the past.

"Nothing. I'm just glad to be here with you."

"Same here."

He rubbed her back, eyes hinting at veiled emotion. Did this mean something to him? Even if it did, there was no ridding herself of her sense of impending finality.

She rested her head against him, falling asleep in his arms.

Chapter Sixteen

Chase

He watched her sleeping form. Once more, she'd fallen back to the secrets. Back into hiding. But her body, it revealed so much. Her patience, like she waited for someone. He knew she hadn't been waiting for him, but for someone who would meet her needs, and he somehow fell into that position. A coldness crept in at the realization she'd never have looked him up, that if not called to task for him, this incredible experience would've passed him by.

He brushed some defiant honey tresses from her face. She looked so serene, angelic. If only he could spare her, from the coming danger, the atrocities that befell her, and her darkest fears. His chest constricted as that familiar protectiveness washed over him.

An all-or-nothing woman. What would she give now that he'd conceded to her wishes? Many women started out sweet, but hid possessive, stiflingly jealous traits. Perhaps not always intentional, just how things sometimes went. Would she do the same?

The more he considered it, the more he figured himself over-analytical about this. He slipped his arm from beneath her head, dressed, then proceeded to the kitchen for some water. There was much to think about, things he didn't want her worrying about.

Mercer intended to stay in his office and sent his family to some distant resort. A well protected one in an undisclosed location. It wasn't his place to question the mans' connections.

This wasn't just a simple case of paranoia. The hacker accessed files relevant to his family and friends, including someone named Jim, Cassidy's employer. Rather, former employer. He didn't have the heart to give her any more bad news.

Within hours of the hack, police found Jim's bullet riddled body near his home, an area not known for such activity. No explanation, no reason, no leads. While anything on her seemed virtually non-existent, it was only a matter of time before dots connected.

He'd pleaded with the Sergeant Major not to tell her yet, explaining everything about her difficulties, and reasoning that she probably couldn't handle the information at this point. Eventually, his argument won out. Not knowing wouldn't hurt her, but knowing might.

He sat at the computer, taking a large gulp of water while perusing his favorite YouTube playlist. He dreaded this sit-and-wait game. No doubt the enemy set sight on this place. If only his memory had returned on its own. Instinct told him time was nearly up.

Regret flooded him. If only someone else had come to his aide instead of Cassidy. Too little too late. As much as he loved having her there, was it worth her life? Assuming they both survived, would she be able to handle him returning to work? Long stretches of time apart? Would she trust him enough stick it out? The anxiety nagged at him and he felt selfish for not considering her long-term needs and wants. He'd never betray her, or jeopardize a good thing. Hopefully she realized that.

After finding an intriguing playlist he clicked play all. Immediately a heavy song about being a master of war droned through the speakers. His mind continued to race.

Would she do everything necessary if this plan did work, and he became incapacitated, or would they both end up dead? Was it too late to teach her how to use grenades? While this place gave them the best chance at survival, he knew the plan was reckless. Being the strategist he was, he'd considered many possibilities, including use of the furniture, suspecting there was a reason the tables consisted of such solid, heavy metal. It would take more than that for them to get out alive.

After a few songs in, he considered rousing Cassidy for round two, but decided against it. While he was quite pleased with himself for sending her into a post-coital coma so soon after she woke up, he didn't want her out the entire day.

A nervous energy crept in, instinct of impending disaster crackled, and he perked his ears. A slight vibration beneath his feet and the familiar sound of a distant, muffled explosion tickled his ears. He rushed for floorboard concealing the button, then the trap door, wasting no time reaching the security room. With a rapid eye he scanned them until he noticed two black vans driving past the gate. Adrenaline spiked.

Chase ripped his way back up to the painting and opened the weapons cache. He grabbed what he could, stored several in the closet, making sure to grab the R1 Remington Cassidy seemed so fond of, a G43 Glock he thought she'd like, and some knives for each of them. With pockets full of ammo and a semi-automatic in his hand, he wasted no time getting to his room.

Slinging the weapon over his shoulder, he shook her.

"Cassidy, wake up!" She groaned in protest and amazed him how naturally sexy she sounded.

Images of what they'd done and ideas of what he wished to do flashed through his mind. Not the time for that. He grabbed her clothes and tossed them beside her.

"Cassidy! Up! Now!" He commanded.

She reluctantly sat up, one arm clinging the blanket to her chest as a protective covering, just barely over those sultry mounds. He gritted his teeth.

"What's the matter, Chase?" When her eyes fully opened, she noticed him armed to the teeth, causing them to widen.

"We have visitors, and I don't think they're friendly."

She dressed hurriedly, accepting the weapons he offered with shaky hands. After storing them strategically across her body she followed him to the cache room.

"Are you sure they can get in here?"

He grabbed some tables and placed them as a barricade in the hall, leaving only a narrow gap between them and the wall. They were heavier than they appeared, and he never thought them to be light to begin with. Another reason he was so surprised when Cassidy brought one to him, trying to help.

"I don't know." Although he could tell she had more questions, she held her tongue.

Seconds later an explosion tore through the room down the hall. She gasped.

"Chase?" She whispered.

He pressed a finger to his mouth and motioned for her to sit. He followed suit, crouching, waiting. Several more explosions tore through the walls, sending dust and debris, leaving a dense cloud hanging, singeing their nostrils. They coughed as loud voices shouted. It was impossible to determine how many.

Cassidy tried to be brave, but hearing them left her visibly shaken. He grabbed a few grenades from the closet and rushed stealthily back. It sounded like a stampede as the intruders drew near. He steadied his breath, prepared his mind, allowing himself to go into what he liked to call 'Wolverine mode'.

Several dark heads rounded the corner. He pried the pin from one of his grenades and rolled it down the narrow space he'd created, never leaving his cover. An explosion, followed by screams. A tuft of smoke floated above his head. More men approached. Cassidy focused on him, clearly searching for a cue for what to do.

He rolled another grenade and waited for the expected outcome. Once he heard it, he inched the table up, close to the edge of the hall. Cassidy copied his motion.

At the edge of the hall he caught sight of the massive hole blown in the far side of the wall in what used to be the living area. More men piled in, joining the few remaining. He estimated their odds as at least fifteen to one and counting. Cassidy's eyes nearly fell out of her head.

"Chase, what do we do?" Terror was evident as she whispered her question.

"Focus. Aim. Shoot. Repeat. Don't get hit."

He readied his semi-automatic rifle. After throwing another grenade at the massive incoming horde of armed, darkly dressed mercenaries. he used the distraction to his advantage and fired. Cassidy tried to keep up, clearly struggling.

If she didn't focus, steady herself, it would cost them everything. A barrage of bullets flew at them, and they ducked.

"Cassidy, focus!" She tilted her head. He handed her a grenade. "Pull this pin, throw, and take cover. Don't hold it. Got it?" Though dazed, she did as instructed. She'd never survive the army, looking as vulnerable as he'd ever seen her.

The smoke had nearly cleared the room and he could see the numbers dwindling. Had they not had that in their favor, this might have gone a whole different way, still could. Still, they found themselves outnumbered. Another wave came through the gaping hole.

"There's too many."

Chase raised his weapon but was out of ammo. It would take more than what he had to deal with the incoming wave.

"Cover me."

"Where are you going?" She sounded close to panic, but obeyed.

He was to the closet and back in less than a second, carrying his M202 Flash. Not a weapon for indoors but it may be their only chance. He knelt down on one knee, steadied himself, aimed, mentally prepared for the recoil, and fired. Despite his efforts, he still fell back as the room lit up like the flames of hell. The remainder scurried into dark corners like rats.

"Move up." He told her.

Again filled with a suffocating cloud of dust and debris, he took in what he could see. About a dozen men remained. Nothing else coming in so far.

A sudden wave of dizziness overtook him and he leaned against the wall. Pain seized every muscle. Panic set in and he knew what was coming. While he expected it, he couldn't stop the overwhelming terror.

To his dismay, more men piled through as jolts of lightning crackled in his head. He looked at Cassidy. As his brain eased into darkness, he recognized that this plan was not the best idea after all.

Chapter Seventeen

Cassidy

The firepower Chase yielded was incredible and she couldn't imagine using that thing. Smoke and flame billowed from both ends of it. What hope did anyone have to stand against that?

She continued to fire, but fear crept over her as several more men came through the massive hole in the side, especially at the realization that Chase had stopped firing. Turning to see him convulsing, she froze. It took a bullet grazing her arm to send her crashing to reality.

She grabbed the massive weapon, nearly too heavy for her, imitated the hold and stance he'd used, and fired at the incoming crowd. The weapon flew from her grasp, landing with a loud clang somewhere behind her. The sheer force it yielded send her on her back. She hadn't noticed the men who'd reached her in the meantime from the sides, one attacking Chase's helpless form, another attempting to subdue her.

A memory of him, younger, in the alley behind the dance club, attacked by his tormentors flashed through her mind. She may not of cared as much for herself, but nobody touched those she cared about. Nobody.

She escaped the strong hold on her, giving a sharp elbow to the head of the massive brute, knocking him down. In less than a second she was on Chase's aggressor, just in time to save him from a knife to the throat, mind on autopilot while issuing a flurry of punches, kicks, and elbows, not stopping until he was down.

She fired at the rest of the men, standing defensively before Chase like a towering fortress. Protective, unwavering. With no time to think, she focused on Chase's words. Just aim and shoot. Aim. Shoot. Repeat. Just like Chase instructed.

Not seeing anyone else, she turned her attention on him. Eyes brimming with moisture, she loosened his clothing, not an easy task while he continued to convulse. When he choked, she turned him to his side, in the recovery position. Everything felt surreal, like she was an outsider in her own body.

When he had nothing left in his stomach, he started muttering. His words came out faint, in rapid succession, she barely made them out. Something about a tree, the desert, then the rambling of a series of numbers. Confusing. Oh so confusing. The smell started getting to her.

Was it normal for a person to speak during a seizure? She'd never heard of it before. Of course, the human mind was a complex thing, impossible to understand. Her hands itched to reach out, comfort him, but she didn't dare, too afraid she might somehow hurt him.

"Oh Chase, I hope you're getting what you need out of this, because it's killing me to see you this way."

A crunching reached her ears, and she peered up as a small group of about six men approached. Was there no end to this? She wondered what was on Mercer's personal computer that would make their enemy send waves of men with nothing more than small artillery. They probably figured resistance would only consist of limited firepower, but because of Chase's background as an agent and military man, he'd be cunning enough to maximize the use of what he had.

Perhaps the info on the weapons cache and underground shelter had been omitted. Or perhaps, Mercer wanted them to hack his computer and left information, like bait, for the hacker. Lull them into a false sense of awareness. What did she know? Trying to get her to understand anything pertaining to government and military was like Greek to her. Might as well be trying to teach her algebra. Would not happen.

The way he'd set things up, it seemed he knew what he was doing, and she didn't dare question him. He'd always been smarter than her, and very strategic. She turned as the crunching sound got closer, facing the men with their guns drawn. She squatted behind a table, still covering Chase, gun in each hand, pointed in their direction.

"Looks like your friend is down for the count. What do you think you can do?" The man's eyes, dark, cold, pinned her in place, taunted her as he gave a look that sent chills down her spine.

She didn't kowtow to intimidation. Refused, always refused, to let fear get the better of her.

"Plenty." She gave her surroundings a quick scan. Not far from Chase was one last grenade. That strange, over-sized weapon was too far behind her to chance reaching for. She cared only for self-defence weapons, that one was beyond her comprehension. And after using it the first time, she didn't want to risk knocking herself out.

The men laughed. Another spoke, a deep voice laced with something beyond sinister.

"We want the information he's hiding, and we think you're privy to it." He took a step towards her and she fired, hitting his neck. He fell to the ground, bleeding profusely. The other men started on her and she ducked, grabbed the explosive, pulled the pin, tossed it. The irony of her handling one of those when her great grandfather had nearly died from contact with one wasn't lost on her.

She peered up. Only two men left standing. She aimed.

"One way or another, we'll get what we want." They encroached on her and she shot, one, two, head, neck, then they went down.

When she finally caught her breath, she scanned the scene before her. Sickening, unbelievable carnage. This wasn't like the movies, what a stroke of luck they survived. Though she knew she wouldn't have if not for Chase. In action, he was like a one man army. Nausea crept in. She fought it vehemently.

"Remind me never to get on your bad side." She mumbled as she looked to his now sleeping form. The pained expression he bore, gone, in its place was a look of calm, serenity. She could almost see the boyish charm he once possessed.

She ran for his room in search of a towel, anything to clean the mess. Finding one, and some clothes, she cleaned him up, then carefully put fresh clothes on him, moving him the minimal amount possible. Once done she collapsed against the wall.

It started to sink in. She never killed anyone before, and here she'd been responsible for many deaths. Knowing it was self-defence didn't take away the guilt. She burst into tears as the guilt washed over her. Knowing it was in the best interest of national security, and that Chase would have probably died otherwise, the moisture seeping from her eyes was impossible to stop.

She felt dirty, and sick. So very sick. She wasn't sure if she wanted to scrub herself for the next five years in the shower, or throw up. Perhaps she would do both.

How did Chase manage these things? He must have had a lot of help. It seemed unfathomable for anyone to get out of a similar situation unscathed. Anyone who did would have to be cold, heartless, inhuman.

Her mind was a jumble of thoughts, face still covered in streaming tears. What would Chase do? Did he have his memory back? Did he mean it when he said he wouldn't play her? If she could trust him with her life, did that also mean she could trust him in everything else?

It seemed an eternity as she watched Chase, unsure of what to think, say, do. Eventually her stomach decided for her. She barely got to her feet before she heaved, over and over, until she had nothing left, but still she continued. It seemed as though her stomach was trying to clear her conscience, but it didn't seem to help.

Chapter Eighteen

Chase

He stood away from the overturned table, noting the carnage. Perhaps he was used to this, but Cassidy wasn't. She hunched over in a corner, heaving. Even though it's self-defence, at the moment it clicks in, it's hard to deal with. Sporadic images from his episode flooded him, and he remembered her defending him.

She'd been nervous at first, overwhelmed, until an enemy was on him, as he went in and out of consciousness after the seizure struck. Then it was like watching a phoenix rising from the flames. Her eyes, he'd never seen them so dark, so consumed with fire, and behind them... He recognized it. A trigger. Before he knew it she was there, and his assailant was staring into the void.

Memories of his youth flooded him. Bullies in and out of school, the attack in the alley behind the club so long ago. While all his other friends stood by in shock she stepped in, stood before him, blocking his assailant from continuing to attack. Friends of the assailant harassed, cursed at, and spat on her, but she didn't waver. She was a stone, taking it all, not even a flinch.

But she was only a teenager, a young girl, too young to have to have to deal with any of that. That was something soldiers developed, part of their training, a reason to fight and keep fighting. It made little sense. The only other possibility was... *Oh God! Cassidy, poor sweet woman. What happened to you?*

All the secrets she held, the emotional detachment and distancing, her strange behavior, anxiety, it all made sense. He'd been a fool not to see it, but it raised more questions. He needed to know what happened to her, how she truly felt, everything. The idea of anyone mistreating Cassidy left his blood boiling.

"Cassidy, are you alright?" He rubbed her back gently.

She wiped her mouth with the back of her hand and stood, turned to face him. The guilt, he recognized it. He knew it would never fully go away, but he wanted to help.

"I... I don't know."

He smiled affectionately, tucking a loose strand behind her ear.

"You were brave." Her eyes widened.

"T-thank you." He caressed her cheek.

"I think we need to talk." Her brows furrowed in fear as though she knew what was coming.

"I don't think that's necessary." She pulled away, and once again that barrier, the walls came up. His anger surfaced.

"NO! You're not going to shy away from me this time, Cassidy! I recognize triggering when I see it. What is it? Tell me!"

She trembled, hesitated, fear radiating.

"Well?"

She cast her eyes to the ground, wracking her fingers.

"My mother..." She was hiding something. He couldn't take the secrecy. She needed to open up.

"Cassidy... Out with it!"

She sighed, looked him square in the eyes.

"You, OK? My mother... and you."

A jumble of emotions swept through him. He ran a hand over the top of his head as a groan of frustration escaped him. He wanted to snap the neck of the prick who'd hurt her.

"I want to know what happened to you. How you feel about me... Years ago, when you told me you loved me, did you mean it?" She backed slowly, apprehension escalating.

"Come on. Tell me. I dare you!" His eyes narrowed.

She shook her head, fighting to maintain her secrecy.

"I can't. I'll just scare you off." Tears formed in her eyes. Perhaps she needed to let it all out.

"I double dare you Cassidy. Let me have it! Everything!"

She let out a cry of anguish and threw her arms up in defeat.

"You want to open Pandora's box? You got it! But don't be mad at me if you don't like what you find." He nodded for her to continue. She heaved a sigh of resignation.

"Growing up, I had it rough. My father was... violent, angry, manipulative." She paced.

"I couldn't understand why anyone would get a beating just because *he* lost something, and somehow it was my fault, or my mothers'. It wasn't just the one thing either." She rubbed her arms against the chill that crept over her. He exercised patience as she continued.

"He'd go through these... phases. Some days he seemed alright, others he would go crazy over little things, like getting marker on the phone while taking a message, or forgetting where he put his chequebook, or dealing with a problem tenant. He'd thrown furniture, anything he could get his hands on." She swallowed hard.

"If anyone was unfortunate enough to cross his path, they'd fall to his wrath. It took little for him to lose it and take it out on those around him. If something didn't go his way, a beating was a potential result, as well as broken objects and busted doors." She took in a shaky breath, avoiding his obvious disdain. How could anyone do this to her?

"It was worse for my mother. Whatever I went through, I'm sure she bore the brunt of it. He was always a selfish man. I was still in the single digits when I found out just how much. I still remember waking up because of my mothers' cries of protest and discovering what was happening, him naked, trying to... and her trying to kick him off... It still haunts me. All my mother could say was that he was never able to take 'no' for an answer."

His stomach churned.

"Then there were the mind games, manipulation. Nothing I did was right. If I studied hard and aced every test, it meant I was cheating." She rubbed her left cheek subconsciously.

"If I talked to a guy on the phone, I was a whore. If he heard my friends and I mention a guy we considered cute, I was hormonal and crazy. Their words." She made her way to a wall, leaned against it, slid to the floor. She wrapped her arms around her knees.

"I defended my mother whenever possible, but couldn't be around all the time, and she wasn't helping either. When I interrupted her beating I'd get my own, followed by her defending him. Every time he did or said anything, whether I defended myself or her, she'd take his part, defend him, and negate anything I did."

She released another shaky breath.

"It got to a point I would sense the worst days because she'd unload on me. Between the two of them, I never doubted that I was some horrible monstrosity. They didn't have any problem telling me straight out. It became so deeply ingrained in my head that I couldn't stand being in my own skin, or the sight of myself, so I cut myself out of every picture."

It took everything not to explode. Pandora's box indeed.

"I once kept a diary where I wrote my thoughts and feelings. A birthday gift from my aunt. One day he read it, didn't like what it said, so he ripped it up in front of me. I wasn't permitted to have one after that."

He swallowed the bile rising in his throat. He wanted to scream, but he'd pushed her to find out, so he forced himself silent, stewing.

"I had no outlet, nobody to talk to at school, no support. I was being bullied there too. So my mother, me, we both suffered in silence, both desired the eternal slumber. I didn't find out until after, but my mother couldn't hold down all those pills, and I was too weak, so I cut."

"Cassidy!" It was too much to take. She shot him a piercing stare, tears clouding her eyes.

"What? You wanted everything, you got it!"

Her head rested on top of her knees. He gulped, his heart bled.

"On the worst days, at night, I would cut myself, make myself bleed. I'd look out at the night sky and cry, asking 'why?'. What had I done to deserve that life? So I'd bleed, anything to release the rage, the pain."

His whole body vibrated. He'd been so blind, so ignorant, but he was young, he didn't know or recognize the signs.

"Do you still..." Her head shot up.

"God no!" Her head returned to her knees.

"What happened when you met me?" A ghost of a smile formed on her face.

"You..." She breathed. "I've never met anyone like you. You held an intelligence and integrity that belied your years. You're the only one, the only man that ever affected me so deeply. In all my oddities and antics, you never seemed to judge. You always appeared slow to speak and quick to listen. It scared me, seemed too good to be true."

She rested her chin on her folded arms.

"You had your oddities, but overall, your character was impeccable. When you were around, it felt like..."

She paused in thought. He held his breath.

"Like I'd been living in the dark all my life and one day this amazing light comes and shines against the darkness. I fought every inclination I had towards you and lost." She rubbed her shins subconsciously.

"When my mother came up with the bright idea to tell my father my guy friends were gay because he was getting out of control again, I didn't want to. At least, not for you. Yet I let my mother do what she wanted. I think my father sensed my feelings though, he sensed something, because he singled you out."

He raised a brow of surprise.

"He would approach me just to insult you, I think he hated you, but I stuck up for you. I wondered if he could see in you the same thing I did. He seemed to have a hatred for anything good. At least, anything that mattered to me."

He sat beside her. His heart ached for her. *Oh God, Cassidy...*

"You didn't need to defend me." She merely shrugged.

"You're an amazing person, Chase. One worth defending. So easy to fall for, so hard to ignore. It's no surprise women want you. You deserve the best of everything and I can't see you settling for anything less."

He ran a hand over the stubble on his head.

"If you felt that way, why did you distance yourself from me? I didn't run away Cassidy, you did."

"I got scared, but in my fear of scaring you off I lost you anyway. When I told you I loved you, it was so hard. I fought over fourteen years worth of demons to do it."

"God, Cassidy. I'm sorry. I didn't know if you meant it, or if it was another dare."

She wiped away a tear.

"No dare, just me, but it doesn't matter, does it? When I said it, you rejected me."

His jaw tensed. He'd been so unsure how to react when she said that.

"I didn't reject you, not really." She rushed to her feet.

"Like hell you didn't! 'You can tell if someone loves you by looking in their eyes.'." She turned to face him, frustration apparent.

"At the very least you were calling me a liar, and I have witnessed enough to get how that's wrong. A lifetime worth. Love's also an action, Chase, not just fuzzy feelings and doe eyes. I've seen people look each other in the eye and lie with a straight face. Then there are people like me, who suffer in silence, and in fear and trembling, face their demons and worst fears, to give their hearts away."

He stared, dumbfounded. She nipped her lower lip.

"Did you ever stop to wonder why I was so much more protective of you? Why I was so ready to take a beating or fight to protect you? Why I enjoyed your company so much? It wasn't because I hated you! Seriously, how many teenage girls would rather stay out late talking to a guy about earwigs, because it meant more time with him?" She let out a heavy sigh.

"But you didn't see it, you didn't believe me. Or didn't care and didn't want to. It would have been easier for me if you'd laughed in my face and ridiculed me. I could have hated you. Or simply told me you didn't reciprocate the sentiment. I'd have accepted that and appreciated your honesty. But you spoke like you heard me, you listened, acknowledged my words, may have shared those feelings, but thought I was lying. That broke me."

Oh shit...

"So I tried so hard to forget. Bury it like everything else and move on. I still had the same demons rattling around in my head, with a new lesson. Just take what I can get. I was so stupid! I met one of the greatest men in the world and made a total fool of myself for someone who didn't want me. Yet, even afterwards, I'd still rip out my heart and lie through my teeth before a group of my peers to try to protect you, even if what you said or did was wrong." She paced once more.

His mind struggled with it all.

He ran a hand over his face. This was so much information to assimilate. It was overwhelming. It sounded so crazy, but he knew Cassidy would never lie to him.

"What do you want from me?"

"What I want and expect are two different things, but the answer to the question is you."

Everything was so overwhelming, confusing. How was he supposed to take this?

"And what if I told you I don't want you around? If I told you to go away, never come back?"

OK, that was a test. He probably shouldn't have asked. The pain in her eyes was unmistakable. Her lips quivered as she trembled.

"You deserve the best Chase. If you want me gone, I'll go."

He stood, paced, ran both hands over his head. It explained so much. She never stopped caring. And when he thought she'd gotten over him so quickly, she'd secretly continued to harbor those feelings. She just considered it hopeless, chalked it up as a lost cause, and tried to move on.

He'd been so ignorant of her trials, her pain. what he'd said that day only contributed to her misery. Guilt tore at his gut. At least she was here now, opening up to him, finally. He couldn't think of anything to say. His mind was in chaos.

This should probably scare him, but it didn't. Just thinking about what she'd been through was enough to break his heart and make him want to butt heads. He wanted to wrap his arms around her, make her feel safe, but feared she'd run from him. This was a delicate situation.

"Is that what you want?" He couldn't answer her. Not yet. His mind still needed to process everything. She'd been through so much...

"I... I need some air." He muttered and rushed out through the gaping hole in the side of the building.

"Chase?" It came out a barely audible whisper. He continued on. He needed to contact the Sergeant Major anyway, and time to think.

Chapter Nineteen

Cassidy

Her body froze in shock. She knew, KNEW it was a bad idea to tell him anything. The sound of an engine roaring to life echoed through the now open room, undoubtedly Chase's great escape. She ran out to see a red car peeling away, a dust cloud in its wake. Mercer must have had one stored away somewhere on premises. Her heart shattered into a million tiny pieces, just like in the park when she was a young, stupid girl. Now she was just a stupid woman. A foolish, stupid woman who hadn't learned a damn thing.

She always thought he was this nice guy. Thoughtful, polite, understanding. How could she have been so blind, so dumb? Had she ever truly known him? She collapsed to her knees, trembling as torrents flooded down her cheeks. That was the answer then. All these years, she'd been right all along. He never cared, only tolerated her, pitied her. As if her mother's failed surgery wasn't enough. Not to mention her home being torched to the ground, her best friends trapped inside...

Time stood still as she remained on her knees. The tears just wouldn't stop.

Everything, everyone that mattered, gone. She had nothing left. Her heart beat so loudly she didn't hear the footsteps behind her. All she knew was a sharp pain in the back of her head, followed by darkness.

"Chase wasn't there." A familiar male voice stated as her foggy brain fought for consciousness. Her fogged mind struggled to figure out where she was, what was happening. All she knew was the distant sound of male voices and the throbbing pain in the back of her head. Slowly she noticed the rope binding her wrists and ankles.

"What do you mean he wasn't there?" This one spoke harshly, with an unfamiliar accent.

Everything was a blur when she opened her eyes, and it took a while to focus.

"Ask the woman." If they thought she would help them, they were barking up the wrong tree. He probably took off to another country just to get away from her. Her chest constricted painfully at the thought.

It took a moment for all her senses to work and realize she sat captive in a chair in the middle of a dimly lit room smelling no better than stale sewage. The only furnishings were a wooden table which held a laptop, large jug of water, and some cups. Around it were a few wooden chairs. Two men stood in the far corner, cloaked in shadow. She sensed their eyes on her, their hatred nearly tangible.

A large hand grabbed a fistful of hair, pulling back painfully. She gasped as she stared right into Aiden's sinister blue eyes.

"Surprised to see me?" She swallowed hard against her fear.

"You could say that."

"Bet you're wishing you poisoned my food now." She refused to show even an ounce of her anxiety.

"Oh, what might have been." She watched his eyes darken with veiled threats. The smirk on his face was equally threatening. Her head burned as he tightened his grip. He hissed through his teeth.

"Why don't you be a good girl and tell me where your boyfriend is?" She gave a weak smile, anything to hide the terror inside.

She'd watched the news enough times to realize what can happen to women who get captured by these types. What did it matter? There would be no hero to save her. She was as good as dead unless she got herself out. It was as it had always been. In a world so cold and ruthless, she was on her own.

"Well gee, as much as I'd love to tell you, your guess is as good as mine."

Aiden delivered a backhand so hard it brought her right back to her childhood. Only this time, she contained venom in her bite. She squared her focus right into his eyes and gave a well practiced smile.

"Wow. You must feel like a *big* man now."

Another backhand, this time harder, and she tasted blood as her teeth tore into her cheek. Both cheeks stung, tingled.

"I suppose that counts as turning the other cheek, right?" In the blink of an eye he had a tactical blade against her throat, so tight it dug in. She shut her mouth. If there was any chance of getting out she'd have to tread carefully hence forth. Let him think her a coward. All that mattered was escape, or die trying.

"Keep mouthing off like that and I'll cut out your tongue." She merely nodded. He must have seen it as her full submission because he smiled, returning the blade to his side. He patted her cheek. Somehow she resisted the urge to spit in his face.

"That's a good girl. Now, one last time. Where's Chase?"

She glared daggers. "As I told you. I don't know. He took off not long before you guys kidnapped me. Didn't tell me where he was going."

He appeared to consider her words before bursting out in laughter.

"I was wondering who'd scare who off first." That cut deep. It took everything she had to hide the pain.

"What can I say? The guy's too stubborn for his own good. He always hated having to rely on people, has a real lack of empathy, not to mention selfish, stubborn, frustratingly opinionated... Now that's a turn off. Had to chase him away. Guy's a total jack off." He laughed again.

She hated herself for this, but whatever lowered Aiden's guard had to be beneficial. It wasn't like Chase cared what happened to her. After telling him about the agony she suffered he just abandoned her. In spite of everything she still didn't hate him, but oh, how she wanted to. At the moment, all that mattered was survival.

"I won't argue with that."

And the Oscar goes to... Inside, she wanted to curl up in a hole somewhere and die. Aiden's tone became serious once more.

"There's still information I want. And I think you can tell me."

She shook her head in dismay.

"Whatever it is, I don't have a clue." Aiden gripped the back of her chair, trapping her under his intense, scrutinizing stare. He leaned in, his breath reeked of stale tobacco, worse than a day old ashtray.

"Tell me if he regained his memory, where the information is, and if his superiors know of it yet."

She was sure he regained his memory. At least based on the seizure and what he muttered during, but beyond that, she had no idea. It wouldn't matter how she answered, if she denied knowledge they'd torture her until they got whatever bogus answer, then kill her. If she told the truth they'd kill her, and probably him too. No matter what, she'd lose, so she remained silent, merely shrugging her shoulders as nonchalantly as possible.

The staring contest lasted only seconds before Aiden growled in frustration and shoved away.

"Lucky for you, I have somewhere to go. But I'll be back. And I WILL have those answers!"

She held her tongue as he and one of the other guys left through a door at the far side of the room. The door slammed so hard the floor beneath her trembled. She gave the room another once over and noticed the covered windows. There was a hallway a way off to her right. How many rooms lay beyond there, she could only guess.

She tugged at the rope binding her wrists, testing them while observing the lone man left behind. He seemed more interested in the gadget in his hand as he tucked earbuds in his ears, connecting them to the small device. Her fingers ran over the knots. As a child she developed a fascination with knots after joining girl scouts. Combined with some of the minor kinky bondage stuff she'd done with a previous ex, knots were nothing to her. Eventually she got free but held her arms behind her, feigning continued captivity.

"Hey!" He didn't seem to hear her.

"HEY!" She nodded as he looked her way. He took out an ear bud.

"I'm thirsty. Can I have some water?"

His reply was merely a long-running series of swears and insults. At least that's what she assumed since she didn't understand what he was saying, only that he looked ready to skin her alive. It didn't pay to play the flirtatious damsel with these guys, not that she was the type, but they'd likely burn her alive for doing it.

"Please, I'm parched." He approached the table and as he left the concealment of the shadows, it was obvious he was every inch a militant. Muscular, armed, and dangerous. She had one shot, along with the element of surprise. Hopefully it was successful. After pouring the liquid into a cup he brought it over to her, but dumped it on her instead.

As he hovered, spewing more of what she assumed was hate-filled curses, she acted. She grabbed his arm and spun him around until his back was facing her. She pulled him toward her, wrapping her free arm tightly around his neck and squeezed, using her shoulder to press against his head while clutching her other shoulder to strengthen the hold. In spite of how fiercely he struggled, in seconds he was limp.

She quietly counted to three before releasing him. In less than a minute she salvaged every usable weapon from his unconscious body and cut free her ankles, even taking what was a dual radio and mp3 player. Afterwards, she bound him with so many knots it would likely take him a week to get out without a knife, and rolled him beneath the table.

Her heart drummed wildly as she made her way to a window and cautiously peeked out, careful not to disturb the black cloth covering. A massive field hedged in by trees lay beyond, and a narrow road ran through.

She was about to pull away when a low rumble reached her ears. It grew louder, and a camouflage painted Jeep pull into view. Aiden sat behind the wheel, his accomplice beside him. Was there anyone else here? Did they guard the field and surrounding area? What kind of security system did they have? She was afraid to find out. In a split-second decision she grabbed the laptop and shoved it in the case hidden behind it, along with the wires, and slung the case over her head and across her shoulders. Mercer may have an interest in it.

She clutched the pistol tightly with one hand, folding knife in the other. Stealth was preferable but if she had to use the gun, she'd be ready. Sucking in a breath she carefully opened the door and peered out. Not a soul in sight, not a sound. She clung to the wall and proceeded quietly to the door to her right.

Her pulse quickened as she approached. She held her breath and pressed her ear against it. Nothing. She opened it slowly.

To her surprise, she found herself in a fair sized garage. The only source of light was a small window on the garage door, which reflected off the black hood of a Hummer. Heart racing, she opened the door of the vehicle, searching until she found a set of keys hiding over the visor. This seemed too easy, too good to be true. So close to freedom she could almost taste it.

She ran to the door, peered out the window. One guy stood nearby, armed to the teeth, wearing all black, head covered by a matching bandanna. Where there was one, there was likely more. She waited, watching. Two more came and went. It seemed they were patrolling. Her heart sank. How would she get out now?

As she returned to the vehicle, the loud creak of the garage door opening startled her. She hopped in, closed the door, replacing the keys before hiding behind the driver seat.

Two men entered. It seemed they were arguing but she couldn't understand what about. Noticing a black tarp beside her, she covered herself quickly. The doors of the vehicle opened, and she clutched her weapons tightly, crouching further against the back of the driver seat. It took all she had to bite her tongue as a large black bag landed on the backseat, inches from her face. Whatever was in it reeked worse than just stale sweat. Her stomach roiled, and she covered her mouth, fighting the urge to vomit.

Oh yeah, this is going to be an interesting ride...

She didn't dare move, didn't dare look out the window. She just crouched there, wondering what was happening. The vehicle stopped once, the driver spoke to somebody, then continued on his way. It was a challenge to keep quiet, especially when their otherwise boring conversation turned to what they wished they could do to her. As if she didn't already have a reason to throw up.

She didn't know if they'd been driving for minutes or hours, but it felt like eternity. It was beyond her understanding how anyone could do this for any reason, for any length of time. Her legs were cramping, and the odor wasn't getting any better. It took all she had not to jump for joy when they finally stopped.

As the men exited the vehicle, she took a chance and peeked out. They were at a gas station in the middle of nowhere. A sign at the edge of the road read 'Portland–20 Miles'. Where the hell did they take her?

Once the two men were inside, she eased out the door facing opposite the store to avoid getting caught. She stored her weapons on her person and bolted to the tree line across the highway as soon as there was a break.

She watched from the safety of lush green forest cover as the two men walked out. This would have been near impossible had it been winter instead of spring. She shivered in spite of the warm air. The forest seemed quiet, not even a chirp, as though even the birds could sense danger hanging in the air.

One man, the taller one, pulled a cell phone from his pocket, pressed the screen, and talked. She saw it before she heard it. His anger, frustration. Instinct told her they'd discovered her escape. They stormed the Hummer, searching every inch.

In a long-winded rant he put the phone back to his ear. She ducked lower as the men scanned the area. By this time her heart beat loudly in her ears and she was sure it would rupture. After several more curses they jumped in the vehicle and rushed back the way they came.

A sigh of relief escaped her as she sank against a tree. Sure, she was alone, homeless, and they would now hunt her to the ends of the earth like some hapless animal, but she was alive. That was something.

It wasn't the first time she'd been homeless, she knew she could adapt. But she never had to worry about looking over her shoulder before, except for Steve. When it came to the threat of danger, Aiden and his men made Steve look like a toddler having a tantrum. Every move she made needed careful planning. One mistake and Aiden would take her life.

She didn't know how much time had passed as she deliberated on what to do. A part of her blamed Jim for this. If not for him, she wouldn't be in this mess. She also wouldn't have been in a situation where Chase could rip her heart out all over again. What a mess this turned out to be.

It took a phenomenal amount of effort not to cry as her demons crept in, taunting her. It was like her childhood all over again. She rose to her feet and walked, keeping within the cover of the forest as she put the tiny music player on. Kesha's voice bellowed about showing her true colors through the ear buds.

The best plan she could come up with was going to her mother's house and contacting the doctor from there. She still somehow had to deal with the burial of her mother. Hopefully Mercer would come through with the remainder of her wage because she needed it. If there was anything left, she was getting the hell out of town. Anywhere away from Portland, Chase and every haunting memory she had of him, and hopefully Aiden and his henchmen.

Chapter Twenty

Chase

"Excellent, we'll get it right away. Does miss Macayla know your memory has returned?" From the look on her face when she helped him to his feet, he assumed she did. Even though she said nothing. He wasn't sure how to feel about that.

"I'm sure she does, though not how much. She didn't ask questions." Not that he gave her the opportunity. He'd cracked her open and took off after she let everything out. He had no intention of abandoning her, and it wasn't like she could go anywhere. But he felt somewhat guilty for leaving the way he did. He needed to assimilate the information, figure out the best way to approach her after that.

"She's smart. Let me talk to her, see what she knows." He mentally kicked himself for the momentary loss of objectivity, he should have been more focused, but she had proven to be every bit a distraction.

"She's not with me at the moment. I'm at the gate right now, assessing the damage." And it was a real mess. The bits of metallic debris spoke of their crude but effective methods. They didn't bother trying to hack it, they just blew it open. "I haven't found anyone else but haven't finished scouring the property yet."

"I'll just call her. At least now we can retrieve the info. Good job on your quick thinking. Doubtful anyone would have considered looking there." He nodded.

"Thank you, Sir."

"Carry on. We'll speak again later."

It took a while to assess the property and piece together an idea of what happened. They busted their way through the gate, drove around the back, and trampled around the side to what they likely perceived as the weakest part of the structure. His mind was still trying to work out details when the sound of his phone snapped him present.

"I can't reach her. It goes straight to voicemail. Is she alright?" He thought about her eye opening confession and figured her upset because he left without giving her an answer. Something he wasn't up for explaining.

"She's probably having a hard time dealing with what happened. I'm sure she'll be fine. Just needs some time to..." He made his way back to ground zero as he spoke and froze. His adrenaline spiked.

A few feet from the hole were the remnants of her cell phone, and a bit of blood spatter on and around the casing fragments. He moved closer, heart drumming wildly. The way the grass lay crushed told him shed either been sitting or kneeling. Large depressions, like boot prints, led away from the area, toward the dirt road which lead to the gate. But he hadn't seen any vehicles.

Whoever it was must probably figured she had information on him. Obviously she did, he saw it in her eyes. Whatever it was, they were determination to get it, and held no scruples against harming women.

He should have stayed with her and just gotten to the bottom of it, her feelings, his feelings, and dealt with it, but instead, he let it overwhelm him and took off like a coward, leaving her vulnerable.

"Chase? What's wrong?" The voice snapped in his ear.

"She's gone." He managed in a whisper. His heart ripped from his chest. If he ever got his hands on the bastard who took her...

"What?!" He cleared his throat. Ice coursed through his veins.

"She's gone."

"What do you mean 'gone'?" He swallowed hard. Why had they taken her? Why not him? Did they think him dead, or gone? He'd driven to the gate, perhaps they noticed him driving away and assumed he left her there alone. Dread filled him. Shit, he screwed up, bad.

"They got her."

Chapter Twenty-One

Cassidy

Finally, the place where it all began. Mercer's office was just a few floors up. It was a miracle she made it, especially when Aidens' lackey's drove by every so often, clearly on the prowl for her. She'd changed her mind, deciding instead to go to her mother's place afterwards. Whatever was on the laptop was likely very important and took priority. She just knew she had to deliver it before anything happened, and her mother wasn't going anywhere.

Looking herself over, she cringed. She was an absolute mess. It had taken all night to get here. She was hungry, tired, and ready to snap. Straightening her hair, she marched into the building.

"Hold on. Do you have an appointment?" The security guard seated behind the desk eyed her with suspicion. It took all she had not to dump the surly man's coffee over him.

"Tell Sergeant Major Mercer that Cassidy Macayla is here to see him. Tell him, it's urgent."

"What's in the bag?" She frowned. If this didn't make it to its intended destination, there could be real trouble. After what she'd been through, she wasn't ready to trust just anyone. The muscular guard rose to his feet. His height, intimidating. She refused to give in to fear.

"I need to inspect that." In seconds he was at her side and unzipping the case.

"It's just a laptop. If you're so worried about it, have him come down here." He reached in to pry it out.

"I have to make sure you're not carrying anything harmful."

"Oh, for God's sake! Just call him down here. Anything happens to this laptop because you screwed with it, and you'll be responsible for loss of potentially vital information. Is that worth your neck?" He stared hard, clearly trying to make her kowtow. She was in no mood, it simply wasn't happening. She rebutted his effort with an icy glare.

"Very well."

Hesitantly, he picked up the phone at his desk and punched in a number.

"We're having a problem. There's someone calling herself Cassidy Macayla here and..." His eyes widened, almost terrified. A frantic sound ripped through the receiver, so loud she heard the edge of frustration. "Yes, she's alone. Yes, Sir. Right away." The man appeared frustrated.

"He will see you in his office right away." His voice was ripe with frustration.

"Thank you." She managed, despite how much she wanted to slap him.

Entering the office, a very concerned Mercer greeted her. Memories of the first time in there wreaked havoc on her emotions, her heart. Remembering how Chases' eyes raked over her body... She fought vehemently to keep the memory from overtaking her. She had to focus. It wouldn't be long before she left town and could forget everything that happened here, forget about him.

"What happened?" She collapsed in the chair before his desk. Her aching legs couldn't hold her up anymore.

"Aiden happened." Confusion emanated from his face.

"Who?"

"Aiden Stephenson. One minute I'm at your safe-house, the next thing I know, I wake up tied to a chair with Aiden breathing in my face." She ran her fingers through the tangled honey-blond mass on her head. A shower was mandatory.

"What did he want?"

"Information. Chase. What he knows. Where he is." That last bit clawed at her heart. She fought to block him from her mind. "They got nothing from me, though."

"How did you escape?"

"Not sure why, but people like to underestimate me. He took off and left only one person to watch me. I hopped in a vehicle and hid in the back. Stopped at a gas station about 20 miles from Portland. While they were inside, I ran to the woods and walked through, staying close to the edge of the highway." She leaned to one side, removed the burden she carried, and placed it on his desk.

"Before I got away, I got this. Don't know if it'll be of any value to you, but I thought you might find it of interest."

He gave a quizzical stare as he unzipped the black, leathery case.

"It's a laptop. Not sure what's on it, but from what I saw, there's at least some important looking documents."

She sat in silence as he opened it up, brought it humming to life. He pressed his lips together.

"It's password encrypted." She frowned.

"Does that mean I wasted my time snatching it?" He smiled.

"No. We'll have it cracked in no time. Thank you for your quick thinking. This could help a great deal."

"I was hoping it would prove useful."

Mercer sat, pensive.

"What did Chase say to you after his seizure? What do you know?" Why was it suddenly everyone wanted inside her head?

"He said something about a tree in the desert and muttered a bunch of numbers. I didn't know if it was code for something, or coordinates on a map. This is your domain, not mine."

His face was grim. Had she said something wrong?

"Did you repeat any of this to Aiden?" She shook her head.

"Not a word." This seemed to appease his concern. "What is Chase exactly? He has two jobs and I don't understand. He was pretty vague when I asked him. I mean he reports to you, yet he..."

"He also works for a division of homeland security. All information tied to that is classified."

It was apparent her question frustrated him. She wouldn't push.

"OK. What am I going to do about Aiden? He knows who I am, and he's been looking for me. It was hell trying to get here while his goof-ball friends were driving around trying to find me, and no doubt trying to find Chase."

He was silent a moment, apparently deep in thought.

"How do you feel about letting yourself be bait?" She glared.

"Chase and I will figure something out. Given your escape, they will be furious and out for blood. With Aiden focused on you, we can use the distraction to sneak in and capture him." Her heart constricted painfully at the mention of his name. "Are you alright?"

She straightened. She could mollify her broken heart later. "I have a funeral to plan. How long will this take?"

"Not long. You need to get washed up. There's a shower in the rehab facility on the first floor. I'll speak with Chase in the meantime. When ready, we'll follow you." Sounded deadly. If she got out of this alive, it would be nothing short of a miracle.

"Alright, but I have no change of clothes."

"You'll have some in about a half hour."

"Very well."

The heat of the shower may have soothed the aches and pains in her muscles, but did nothing to ease her fatigue. A long yawn escaped her. The least they could do was let her sleep first. After rinsing, she stepped out to see a fresh towel and new clothing on the bench of the change room, a small piece of paper with just her name scrawled on top.

After putting on the bra and panties, she examined the clothing. A soft pink, form fitting, long sleeve blouse with hip-hugging blue jeans. Only after the shirt was on did she notice how low-cut it was. While it didn't reveal everything, it certainly showed enough to draw attention. She walked to the floor-length mirror at the end of the row of lockers.

Oh, it would definitely get Aiden's attention, and likely that of every man within viewing distance. She never owned an outfit that flattered her form so well. How much attention had the Sergeant Major been paying? All she could do was shake her head while holding back a giggle. He must get his wife to do his shopping.

Upon entering the familiar office, a noise to her side caught her attention. She turned. Her heart skipped as Chase's eyes consumed her in a slow, hungry scan. She fought the jolt traversing her spine and swallowed. He didn't want her, it had all been a lie. And like the fool she was, she gave him exactly what he wanted. He just wanted to use her body, nothing more. She forced her attention back to Mercer.

"So what are we doing? Will I get to nap first? I'm exhausted."

The two men exchanged glances. What had they been talking about prior to her arrival?

"I'll drive you to your mother's place. We'll keep an eye on you from unmarked vehicles. When you're ready, make yourself seen. We believe Aiden knows of the location so when you make your presence known, we'll be ready to act." She nodded in acknowledgment.

"Did you find anything on the laptop yet?" Mercer shook his head.

"It's still a work in progress." She didn't push any further.

When she got there, she retrieved the key taped under the mailbox and let herself in. She didn't bother changing, just jumped in the bed, placing her weapons in the drawer of the nightstand beside her. Seconds after her head hit the pillow, she was out.

Her eyes sprang open. Had something woken her? Darkness was all encompassing. She checked the alarm clock on the nightstand next to the bed. Nine o'clock. Apprehension filled her, a sense of looming danger.

Thoughts of Chase filled her. She shouldn't still want him after that outright rejection. She knew she should move on. There was no other choice. Her mind flip-flopped between wanting to kiss him and kill him. Just remembering the way his eyes worked over her earlier set her insides on fire. Clearly, something was wrong with her head. With a groan she sat up.

"Finally awake, Sleeping Beauty?" She sucked in a breath as her eyes adjusted to see Chase on the rocking chair in the corner. Even in the dark, there was no missing his predatory stride as he stood and approached.

"What are you doing in here? Were you watching me sleep this whole time?"

"Nah, only about twenty minutes."

She didn't know why it didn't scare her. Probably should have.

"Why aren't you in your unmarked car?" *And hiding from me...*

"I'd rather be in here." She frowned.

"Don't worry about me, Chase. I'm a big girl and can take care of myself. You don't need to be..."

"I'm sorry. I shouldn't have left you behind. Shouldn't have taken off while you were still so vulnerable. If I had been smart..." Guilt dripped from his voice, framing every word. He wasn't here because he cared, he was here because he felt guilty. Her heart broke again. He sat beside her on the bed. She stood as his hand skimmed her shoulders. It was difficult to brush off what stirred inside, but it needed done. She grabbed her weapons and concealed them on her person.

"Don't worry. I'm fine." She adjusted the weapons concealed beneath her clothing while making her way to the door.

"Cassidy..."

"I said I'm fine. You don't need to apologize." She opened it, Chase followed. "If that's why you're here then you can just forget about it. Go back to your vehicle and watch from there." She made her way to the kitchen, flicking on the light.

"That's not why I'm here." His voice was gruff, edged with irritation. She flung her arms up dismissively, turned, leaned against the cream colored granite counter, arms crossed.

"Then what? You want to watch me make a fool of myself again? I won't be spilling anymore secrets or emoting all over you like last time. Final mistake, I assure you."

His expression was soul-rending. One would think she'd ripped his heart out. Unfortunately for him, she knew better. Her eyes were wide open. He was ruthless, cold, like ice.

"It wasn't a mistake! Just a lot of information to take. You've been through so much." There it was, the pity. What she didn't want or need. He continued before she could speak. "And when they got you... Hell, I can see the hand prints on your cheeks. It kills me!"

She stiffened.

"Not your problem, and I've dealt with the like before. He didn't get the chance to break me." He blinked, jaw tensed.

"Don't retreat inside your shell again, please! Cassidy, I didn't run from you, I only needed time to let it sink in. It sounds so..."

"Crazy?" He nodded. She groaned.

"You dared me to give up my secrets, reveal my heart. Acted like it was life or death. When I did, you asked what my response would be if you didn't want me around, then drove off like a bat out of hell. It doesn't take a genius to realize you were running scared. The only reason you're here now is because you feel responsible for what happened. Coupled with that, Aiden possibly getting information from me troubles you."

He opened his mouth, but she refused to let him weasel his way out of this one. She wanted to scream, rage, throw things. Anything but let him see her cry.

"You don't need to worry, Aiden didn't get a damn thing. Your secrets are safe. And I already told you if you don't want me around I won't make a fuss. Your departure spoke volumes, and as you can see, I'm fine, so go. I know it's what you want. When this is over, you'll never have to see or hear from me again." The idea choked the air from her lungs but she wouldn't cave to the pain, nor the dam behind her eyes ready to burst.

He deliberated for a moment. What was the problem?

"Is that what you want? You want me gone? After how you said you never stopped caring for me, that I was so fucking unforgettable, you just retreat into your tough-as-nails shell to lick your wounds?"

He took off on her! What sort of mind games was he playing? Whatever it was, she wasn't biting.

"Screw you, Chase."

He stepped closer. The room heated to a stifling degree. His piercing eyes bore into her, his jaw set. How he looked, how his dark blue shirt hung from those broad shoulders over his muscular physique, all threatened to fog her brain. His voice came out like silk etched in steel. His hands balled into fists, eyes reflecting fire.

"Let me tell you *my* confession, *sweetheart*." Her eyes narrowed. "I never forgot about you either. Wondering whatever happened to you, why you just seemed to fall off the face of the earth. How you could tell me you love me, then give up, move on..." He snapped his fingers mere inches from her face, causing her to flinch. "Just like that. Hell, I even remember the day we met, and now that I have the answers I've always wanted, you want to jump ship because you think you're so damn scary that I'd run away the moment I find the skeletons in your closet." He remembered the day they met? How could that be?

No, it had to be a trick.

"Actually, you drove away." Those searing blue orbs pinned her in place, and the way he licked his lips as he looked her over had her losing her resolve.

"If I wanted to be away from you, I wouldn't be here right now." She swallowed.

Could he be telling the truth? How badly she wished he was. She scanned his features, searching for any hint of deception. Meanwhile he inched closer.

"How can I be sure you mean it and aren't trying to appease a guilty conscience?"

"You need to trust me."

"But..." His mouth swallowed her rebuttal as it captured hers. His lips, his tongue, searching, searing, conquering.

The rush of liquid heat through her body, the fogging in her brain, it was like a drug. Her lungs struggled for much needed air, but his desire for conquest was unrelenting. Her arms rested against his chest as he ran his fingers through silken honey strands, grabbing a handful, tugging for deeper access. She closed her eyes, free-falling in a dark world of promise and sensations, of sweet surrender.

He released her, leaving her struggling to catch her breath. There was no doubt now he'd done this to shut her up. Anger simmered beneath. He cradled her head, gently tilting so their eyes met.

"I love you." Did she dare believe? He must have seen the doubt in her eyes. "I mean it Cassidy! I love you, I think I always have, and I'm sorry it took all this time for me to realize it." She couldn't speak. He really loved her! He went in for another kiss, she leaned toward him, heart drumming in anticipation. A few solid pounds against the door, followed by a deafening crash shattered the moment.

They rushed for the back door at the other side of the kitchen, throwing on her sneakers on the way. Not seeing anyone, they ran out into the cool darkness, closing the door behind them. She retrieved the gun at the side of her waist. Chase did the same.

"I've never seen you carry before." She whispered.

"Only under certain circumstances." He crooked that wicked grin that made her stomach twist in knots.

They crouched against the house, inching around, using the surrounding bushes for concealment in the darkness. Reaching the front, she scanned the street. Where were the undercover cars? She couldn't see any vehicles, and nothing beyond the lights of the street lamps.

"Didn't Mercer say he'd have undercover vehicles watching the place?"

"He does. They're parked further away to avoid detection."

"I see..."

"She's not in there!" A familiar voice drew near. Aiden!

"She is, I saw her through the window." Another man, similar build, but taller, with dark hair and a voice like thunder.

Chase fell back a few bushes behind her, silently urging her to follow. His plea was urgent. She didn't understand why until it felt like the back of her head was on fire as something dragged her out onto the lawn.

"There you are." With a quick spin she sent an elbow to his side, driving the air from his lungs, but his hold didn't loosen. She grabbed the hand on her head and with the other, leaned in and punched, before sending her knee driving into his abdomen. When he lost his hold, she flipped him to his back, and backed away quickly, pointing her weapon at him.

She didn't have time to catch her breath as a strong pair of hands grabbed her arms tightly, pinning them behind her back. She stomped on a large foot, whipped her head back, only to meet a solid wall of muscle. Why wasn't Chase doing anything?

The Goliath of a man grabbed her weapon, but she refused to give up. She spun, squirmed, kicked, anything to make contact and inflict pain, but her captor only laughed. After rising to his feet, Aiden glared.

"You're too stubborn for your own good." Aiden quipped, eyes devouring her. "Are you always this feisty?" The way the question rolled off his tongue sent cold shivers down her spine. She renewed her efforts, but it was a waste of time.

"After your crafty escape, did you really think I'd come unprepared?" She fought the urge to look for Chase. If Aiden didn't know he was there, she didn't want to tip him off.

That proved a waste of effort as he seemed to see past her eyes, in her thoughts. He took a gun from his side and shot into the bushes, the entire length of the house. She jumped, pools forming behind her eyes as she looked, a deadly cocktail of anger, frustration, and helplessness swam in her head, in her veins. Every muscle tensed, burned.

If Chase was dead, Aiden would pay with his life. No signs of blood, no movement. It was so dark perhaps they wouldn't have noticed if he were bleeding. Where had he gone? Was he injured, dead? Had he gone for help? She felt cold, numb. He was getting help, had to be.

Her reaction seemed to speak louder than she'd intended.

"Chase is here somewhere. Find him!" His voice came out loud, angry. Cassidy fought to put on a brave front. "You made a big mistake taking that laptop. Was it worth your life?" She glared.

"You were planning to kill me anyway. Why insinuate otherwise?"

His mouth curled into a heinous grin.

"Are you going to tell me what Chase knows, or do we have to do things the hard way? Believe me, the hard way is more painful, for you."

Was anyone in the neighborhood seeing this, or were they all so preoccupied with their own lives to care?

"I told you, I don't know anything." He stared, eyes telling her he didn't believe her.

"Where's the laptop?"

"I don't have it." He approached, his eyes, his expression, a warning.

"Tell me where it is." This was it, her last day on earth. Where was Chase, and the promised help?

"I don't have it. You're wasting your time." He eyed her with scrutiny, assessing her. He punched her square in the jaw, hard enough to draw blood as her teeth bit into her lip.

"You turned it in, didn't you?" Her silence was all the response he needed, and he punched her again, like a sledgehammer, so hard she slumped against the solid wall of muscle that was her captor.

Pain radiated. Colors sparkled before her eyes as she looked up, mingling with the stars, and she fought the ringing in her ears. "You bitch!" He let loose once more, and she fell to the ground as the vice-like grip on her arms gave way.

"Jim thought he could interfere in our operation, thought he was so clever to send an amateur into something she had no business getting involved in." He kicked her ribs, pain exploded across her side. "Look where that got him."

His words barely made it to her ears. Jim? *Oh no...*

"What... what have you done?" She sputtered against the pain. His expression curdled her blood.

"I'm surprised they never told you. Your old pal got turned into Swiss cheese. Or should I say, your old boss? When I saw the connection between Jim and Mercer, I didn't realize until investigating further, just how connected you were to this whole thing. But my mistake was thinking you were only there to monitor Chase's health and that I could intimidate you, extract any kind of info from you." He shook his head with a cynical laugh.

"It seems I underestimated you. After what you did to my man, and your clever escape, you are either very brave..." He kicked her, forcing the air from her lungs. A groan escaped her. She moved to get up but the beast of a man behind her held her down. "... Or very stupid. And taking the laptop..." He shook his head once more, a laugh of disbelief issuing from his lips.

"I find it hard to believe anyone would have had the foresight to tell you to take it, to realize we'd get you. I mean, they couldn't even tell you about your dear old boss."

She glared as she inched away from his menacing stance. Why hadn't they told her? And after she'd told Chase not to lie to her. A part of her figured he'd been trying to protect her somehow, by withholding the information. If that were the case, did he ever plan to tell her? She knew this was a ruse to get into her head. She was familiar with mind games.

Ever so slowly she ran her fingers down her leg, toward the hem of her pants where her knife lay hidden. There was no way they'd let her leave with breath in her body, and none of the help promised was anywhere in sight. She'd have to fight. If only she'd have known the trouble he'd be when she first saw him walk into Chase's house.

"You're still not getting your laptop back. And I don't know where it is now, so you can either leave me alone or I'll have to rearrange your face after all."

As Aiden laughed she retrieved her weapon, stabbed the man behind her as he reached for her. Quick, repeating, unrelenting. She spun behind the massive brute as Aiden aimed, shot. The man went down. At this point she wished she knew how to throw knives.

"I'm thinking stupid, not brave." He ground out.

"Wouldn't be the first to tell me that." It took effort to scan the perimeter with only her peripheral. Would she be able to make it to the back of the house without getting shot? It didn't seem so.

"I have no doubt."

A loud banging sound from inside the house caught her attention, as well as Aiden's. When he turned to peer in the nearby window, she spun, sprinted, only to have something wrap around her ankle. She fell forward, landing on her hands and knees. How was that oversized bohemian still alive? Aiden was on her in seconds.

"Unfortunately for you, I want you alive. At least, for the time being. You still have info that I want, and you're not getting away like last time." He cracked the butt of his gun over-top of her head. Her head spun, pain exploded. She collapsed. In the distance shouting erupted, electricity crackled in the air, followed by a hailstorm of bullets as she floated into darkness.

"Cassidy? CASSIDY!" The sound came through the fog of her brain as Chase's concerned voice echoed in her aching head. She opened her eyes to see several armed men in black body armor hovering. Chase knelt to her side, face bruised and a bit bloody, but otherwise fine.

A commotion close by drew her attention.

"That fucking bitch! When I get out, I'll kill her!" A loud thud sounded, followed by a long string of curses proceeding from Aiden's mouth.

"You have the right to remain silent. I suggestion you use it." A firm, gentle hand brushed the side of her stinging face. She hissed slightly, trying not to recoil from his touch.

"Chase? You're OK!" She managed through the metallic taste in her mouth. It felt like the bones in her face had shattered. She reached with rubbery arms around his neck, and he pulled her gently to a seated position.

"Of course! I didn't abandon you. I saw what we were up against and signaled for reinforcements." He drew her close, her head pressed lightly against the solid strength of his chest when more shots rang out. She peered up in horror as blood rushed from Chase's face, neck, shoulders. The heavily armored men moved quickly.

"Up there! The attic!" One shouted. She looked in the direction one of them was pointing. In the window of her mother's attic stood a masculine form holding a gun with a long barrel, cloaked in darkness.

"I thought you guys had the place secured!" One man glared at each of the others, voice resounding with authority.

"We did!"

"Then where the hell did he come from?"

Meanwhile Chase fell back. She knelt over him, ignoring her body's searing pain as she moved, trying to cover what wounds she could to slow his bleeding.

"Chase? No!" Tears stung her bruised cheeks.

"Is there something we should know about this place?" One man asked firmly, clearly short on patience.

She struggled for reason in the chaos that ensued. Other men rushed to Chase's side.

"Th-there's an alcove in the attic where my mother used to store her valuables. It's big enough for a grown man to squat in."

"We saw nothing like that in our search."

"You wouldn't, it's hidden behind a bookshelf." She shuddered. That meant the person up there had probably come before she did and spent a great deal of time investigating her house. Her blood ran cold at the idea that he'd been there while she slept.

She returned her focus on Chase, who was bleeding profusely. He reached his hand up to her face.

"Cassidy..." He managed before he fell unconscious.

"Chase!" She was a mess of emotion. Anger, despair, the faintest glimmer of hope. He would be alright. He had to be. She couldn't accept anything else.

"Get up there and take him down!" One man nearby ground out. Several men rushed to obey.

There was no telling how long it had been. Seconds, minutes? She didn't know. An ambulance arrived and two medics rushed from the vehicle with a gurney and equipment to Chase. Before she knew it, they'd put him in the back. She peered down. So much blood.

Everything felt surreal. This couldn't be real. It had to be a nightmare. The whirlwinds of fate wouldn't have thrown them together just to take them apart again, would it?

"I think you should go too." She peered up at the massive standing muscle in black before her. It unnerved her that they were all covered head to toe so that she couldn't even see their faces. Only an intense pair of dark eyes stared back.

With their cut physiques, powerful weapons, and dangerous demeanor, it was enough to instill fear in anyone, giving alluding to the idea of invincibility. "To the hospital. You should get checked out to make sure you don't have broken bones. It looks like that guy really did a number on you."

Perhaps he was right. Besides, she wanted to see Chase, make sure he was OK. He had to be. Her heart pounded in her brain. She wanted to wake up. She didn't dare pinch herself. The last thing she wanted was for this to be real.

"Yeah, I guess."

"Do you want me to call another ambulance?" She shook her head.

"No, I can just ride along with him." At least she didn't have to worry about Aiden anymore. Just a funeral. And Jim... What would she do? No job to look forward to after this. He'd been a kind friend to her, not only her boss.

No family, no friends, no job, no home. If this wasn't rock bottom, she didn't know what was. She sauntered to the back of the ambulance.

"I want to ride with him." She peered at his bloodied form, trying desperately to maintain composure. Knowing she wasn't the only one in the world suffering didn't make it feel any better, especially when everything was still so fresh. All she wanted to do was fall apart. The small, brown haired woman looked on her compassionately.

"Sure, but you must wait until we get to the hospital to get looked at. His needs are more pressing. So be quiet and stay out of the way." Cassidy nodded and sat quietly on the small bench.

In seconds the door closed, and off they went. She watched as the woman and large man worked feverishly to preserve Chase's life. They were still fighting for his survival after arriving at the destination. She watched as they rushed him past a set of automatic double doors at the back of the crowded emergency room. The woman from the ambulance turned to her.

"Sorry, Hun, but you can't follow."

Her eyes burned. She didn't want to leave his side. The brunette must have read her thoughts. She hadn't even the time to protest.

"We'll do all we can." With that, they left.

She sat in one of the cold chairs lining the center of the room, avoiding curious stares, staring at the doors he'd gone through.

"Do you need some help, miss?" A tall blond nurse stood over her, watching expectantly, concern etched on her face.

Before she could respond the loud speakers crackled overhead.

"Code Purple in Emerge two, I repeat, Code Purple in Emerge two. Implement Code Orange..." She didn't get to hear the rest. The nurse by her side started issuing orders. She could have sworn the woman was ready to panic, but held a semblance of calm. It had been a while since she'd heard the term, and it took a moment to remember. *Oh no... Chase!*

"Everyone, please calmly make your way to the exit." Cassidy stood, watching the sea of confused faces.

"What about Chase?" She was ready to leap out of her skin. Confusion transformed the nurse's features.

"Who?"

"The person I came with in the ambulance. Chase Averey. Multiple gunshot wounds?"

"I'll look into it. Just go. Another nurse will lead you to the designated safety zone." She was about to protest further but the nurse rushed beyond the doors where Chase had gone.

Her skin prickled. She wanted to rebel, to follow. The sound of the crowd behind her slowly hushed as the room emptied. She took two steps toward the door when a roar from beyond ripped through the air. Walls shook, pieces of debris fell from above her head.

Glass from the doors shattered, sparkling shrapnel flew toward her. She dropped quickly, covering her head protectively, huddling beside a chair. Raising her head, she peered down the corridor, past other chairs, a nurse's station, to a line up of several rooms. When the dust settled, she stood, rushed in, debris crunching beneath her.

Where was Chase? Her heart pounded in her brain, her feet couldn't move fast enough as she rushed from one corridor to the next, past several bodies. She felt lost. Smoked billowed through the halls as flames licked up the walls.

"Oh Chase, where are you?" She whispered aloud. *Don't cry Cassidy, don't, not yet. He will be fine, he has to be.*

She crashed into the nurse she'd previously spoken to while rounding a corner.

"I thought I told you to follow the others to the designated safe zone." The woman had a few scrapes and bruises, but appeared otherwise unharmed.

"I want to find my boyfriend." The nurse let out an exasperated sigh.

"Follow me, but hurry. We can't stay." She followed the nurse around the corner, down another hall to a room at the end. In the slot on the door was a form with his name on it. "They're getting ready to evacuate him too, and air lift him to a different hospital." As the woman spoke another explosion blasted the door open, and the room erupted in flames. Her body froze, heart at a standstill, so numb from shock she didn't notice as a shard of metal sliced a deep gash in her arm.

Her legs trembled, then buckled. *No...*

"We need to get out of here, now!" Another explosion, and the ceiling started to collapse. Flames, sparkling, crackling, punched through the walls, sending clouds of ash into the air. The nurse pulled her up and they ran, ducking away from falling debris. "Come on, let's go."

Tears burst from her eyes as she raced past rising flames and small explosions, following the nurse in agonizing silence. How was she supposed to come back from this? All she could hear was the beating against her chest, her rapid breathing, and the crunching beneath her feet.

Time stood still, her mind raced. The last thing that mattered in the world to her, gone, just like that. Smoke and ash filled her lungs. A part of her wanted to stay in that hospital as it fell to the ground, let it take her with it, but something drove her on. Perhaps a stronger urge to live, survive, in spite of everything. She couldn't be sure. But she ran, ran toward that exit with all that she had, as everything behind her burned, fell into destruction, chaotic oblivion.

She lunged past the nurse into the open air, lungs welcoming liberation from the toxicity of the hospital air. She hunched over, coughing, sucking in as much air as she could. Dizziness overwhelmed her. It was then she noticed the blood gushing down her arm.

She peered up to see Sergeant Major Mercer standing above her. She couldn't speak. Meanwhile gasps of shock erupted around her. Nurses and doctors gathered around, fussing over her arm. She collapsed, fighting to remain conscious. The last thing she heard was Mercer's voice as he knelt by her side.

"Miss Macayla, don't worry. Everything will be alright."

If only she could believe that. She knew better as she faded into darkness. Everyone she loved, everything that mattered, all taken from her. Nothing would ever be right again. Her lips curled in the faintest smile. At least maybe now she would reunite with them, her family, friends. The thought of seeing them again encompassed her as everything turned to black.

Chase and Cassidy's Song List

Moon and Back – Savage Garden

Crush – Garbage

Until September Ends – Green Day

Schism – Tool

All That I'm Living For – Evanescence

Heart Attack – Demi Lovato

Face The Pain - Stemm

I Swear – All 4 One

Irresistible – Jessica Simpson

Indestructible – Disturbed

Rude Boy – Rihanna

Everybody – Rudenko

Stricken – Disturbed

Partition – Beyonce

True Colors – Zedd, Kesha

Darkest Part - RED